AF622145

INDIA'S UNIQUE TRANSFORMATION PROGRAMME

Solutions to move India in the top ten of the UN Human Development Index

INDIA'S UNIQUE TRANSFORMATION PROGRAMME

(Advanced, comprehensive, integrated, powerful, extraordinary, progressive, innovative, drastic and complete, hence *Unique*)

By

Jasveer Singh
Visionary Architect

© Author
All rights reserved. No part of this book may be reproduced, stored, adapted, or transmitted in any form or by any means, electronic, mechanical, photocopying, micro-filming, recording or otherwise, or translated in any language, without the prior written permission of the copyright owner and the publisher. The book is sold subject to the condition that it shall not, by way of trade or otherwise, be lent, resold, hired out, or otherwise circulated without the prior publisher's written consent in any form of binding or cover other than that in which it is published.

The views and opinions expressed in this book are author(s) own and the facts reported by them have been verified to the extent possible, and the publishers are not in any way liable for the same.

ISBN : 978-93-5128-122-1

Price : ₹ 460

First Published, 2015

Published by

Kalpaz Publications
C-30, Satyawati Nagar
Delhi-110052, Ph. : 9212142040
E-mail: kalpaz@hotmail.com

Laser Typesetting : Future Computer, Delhi
Printed at : G. Print Process, Delhi

Cataloging in Publication Data—DK
Courtesy: D.K. Agencies (P) Ltd. <docinfo@dkagencies.com>

Singh, Jasveer , author.
India's unique transformation programme : advanced, comprehensive, integrated, powerful, extraordinary, progressive, innovative, drastic and complete, hence unique / by Jasveer Singh.
pages cm
ISBN 9789351281221

1. Quality of life—India. 2. India—Economic policy. 3. India—Social policy. I. Title.

DDC 306.0954 23

Solutions to move India in the Top Ten of the UN Human Development Index from the current 135th position within five to eight years

That all the citizens deserve, expect and require from their elected representatives, and is 100 per cent possible.

Recommended as essential reading to all the citizens, especially:

- current and future elected representatives at the national, state, district and village level;
- administrative personnel at the national, state, district and village level;
- management students, practicing management and other professionals;
- young students; and
- remaining adult population eligible for voting.

Perspicacious analysis, marvelous and effective strategy, techniques, formulae, processes, priorities, goals, solutions, projects and tasks for 100 per cent success.

Dedicated to the
Almighty Creator of the Universe

Contents

Editor's Note

(How to Read this Book)

This book is a presentation by an accomplished person and is based on practicality and real data and authority over subject matter. The author reiterates several times only because reiteration is required in the context and reader is advised to sequentially read each word of the book, and the reiterations so as to realize its implications. The book does not only address what is to be done but also how much is to be done.The suggestions presented by the author are not prescriptive but what any normal country should aspire for, in essence these are interventions for the welfare of the people taking into account the population and diversity of the country, and are not exclusive. Any welfare intervention made in a country like ours with its splendid demography can have a multiplier effect just as a small amount of credit introduced in the economy has a multiplier effect. If these interventions take place as they should take place then what the author envisions is actually a normal outcome for a blessed and a truly deserving country like ours, anything short of it cannot be accepted.

Jai Bharat!

About the Author

Mr. Jasveer Singh, currently based in Belgium, is a Visionory Architect. He is from UP, has an M. Tech degree from IIT Delhi and Executive Master of Management (Post Graduat en Gestion) from Ecole de Commerce Solvay, Brussels with about 30 years of senior-level international experience. He speaks some European languages (French, Dutch and German).

After living about 30 years in India, the author has lived with his family for about the same total period in other countries which are France, Australia, Belgium and Germany. During this period, he has also visited about 25 countries for work. This way, he has seen and observed closely the differences in the living standards of majority of people in India and the countries mentioned above. The foreign countries where he lived provide the best facilities in all the domains to the people living there. This helps people to develop their talents and contribute to their nations' as well as their own development and progress. Also, compared to the experiences in India, there are strikingly impressive, smooth, simple, easy and hassle-free administrative processes/services for everybody in these countries, e.g., to get passport, identity card, driving license, rail-reservation, child admission to school, etc. Even more strikingly, all this is done without any extra payment over the officially prescribed charges and without any wheedling-obliging relationship with the service providing administrative staff. And similarly, many other excellent services are provided like 24-hours electricity, water and gas supply, transport, medical, shopping, sports, banking facilities, etc., without any discrimination based on caste, religion or social status. Another major difference: fixed prices everywhere, no bargaining for prices anywhere making the life very simple and easy.

The author has immense desire to see that all the best facilities in all the domains are provided to all the people in India at all the places that will be especially splendid for the children, majority of whom have a variety of talents which can be fully blossomed by using these facilities. If children get the best facilities in the fields of education, sports, culture, arts, music, etc., they can excel in sports and bring hundreds of gold medals in sports events like Olympics, become top-class scientists or medical professionals and get tens of Nobel prizes in commendable fields (not fields regarding child labour or poverty, nor awards on films about slums, etc.,) and become top class musicians and win international awards, etc. A fine example of the use of the magnificent facilities in the developed countries is his son, who by selecting the best institutions according to his interests, aptitude and capabilities has become an accomplished international concert pianist (see www.seenusingh.com). The author wishes similar success to all the children in India which is only possible by implementing "India's Unique Transformation Program" described by him in this book.

Contact by e-mail: jsingh@live.be

Preface

Challenge to Indian political leaders—are they competent, capable, desirous, and willing to fulfil the real deserved needs, hopes and aspirations of all the citizens everywhere in India?

This book presents, after a brief introduction, a critical, factual analysis of the prevailing situation in India with an insight about the reasons and causes of the difficult living conditions of majority of people in spite of the availability of plenty of resources in India—both natural resources and talented human resources. Then, a magnificent vision for the nation and all the population is presented – vision of moving India in the top ten of the UN Human Development Index from the current 135th position within about 5 to 8 years. For achieving the visionary goal, a unique transformation programme of about 100 very huge projects and solutions with their strategic implementation details is discussed. The transformation programme is unique because it has the following exceptional attributes: it is advanced, comprehensive, integrated, powerful, extraordinary, progressive, innovative, drastic and complete. Thus the core theme of the book is this ambitious unique transformation programme which needs to be implemented and is 100 per cent possible to implement to achieve the cherished vision. The implementation strategy with very effective solutions, formulae, processes and techniques that are based on already available, well-implemented, proven models in the developed West European countries is presented in detail which can be used for miraculously fast and balanced development in India to raise the living standard by about 100 times of 100 per cent of the population living everywhere in India.

The book is destined and recommended for all the adult citizens, especially the following categories of people:

- All the current and future-aspirant elected members of Lok Sabha, Vidhan Sabha, Rajya Sabha, Vidhan Parishad, Nagar Nigam, Municipality, Panchayats etc. to help them understand the integrated solutions needed for balanced development of India and learn the techniques to apply for implementing the required technological and management systems – in this regard the book acts as their practical guiding manual.
- All the administrative personnel at the national, state, district and village level so that they are aware of different systems and subsystems needed at different levels for progressive and drastic improvements and they know how effective management can be done at all the levels.
- All the management students and practicing management professionals to expose them to the best management jobs to manage the country so that they can mold the destiny of about 120 crore people and lead the country in the desired direction of development – in this regard the book inspires and tries to persuade them to enter politics for the welfare and uplift of their co-citizens.
- All the young students of India to make them aware of the requirements and challenges of the balanced development of India through the unique transformation program for their bright future so that they get inspired to study management and take up political careers to produce educated, effective political management leaders.
- All the remaining adult population of India who are eligible for voting to elect their representative for the different entities at national, state, city, village level, so that the people become aware of what excellent treatment and facilities they deserve and should demand from their elected representatives in all domains.

Jasveer Singh

1

Introduction

India's bright, dazzling, splendid future?

The present situation in our beloved country is that we are amongst the best in the world in some areas and at the same time, we are amongst the worst in some other aspects. We are at the topmost of the list of countries in the areas where it is a shame to be at the topmost and we are at the bottom of the list of countries in the areas where it is a shame to be at the bottom.

At present, India's position is such that if there was a Nobel prize for corrupt and selfish, some of our citizens would get it every year without break for the last about 50 years, and hence, we are at the top in the list of corrupt countries. Also, we are at the top for hunger, child malnutrition, poverty, crime, black-money, tax-evasion, disrespect to women and girls with extensive scarcity of safety for them (the girls are not even allowed to be born! and if born, they are subjected to heinous crimes!). We are the best in human talent, hard-work and entrepreneurship, and hence we are the best in providing the cheapest labour, be it manual (labourers) or mental (information technology, software, etc.) to the whole world. We are the best in not returning the benefit of the hard work of the entire population to all our citizens by denying them the world's best facilities in all the areas – housing, education, transport, health, sports, entertainment, security, infrastructure, employment, etc. We are the best in not utilizing our natural mineral resources and human talent resources for the benefit of our own nation and citizens because we do not engage seriously in the activities of research and manufacturing of advanced technology equipment and we are the best in draining these resources out of the country almost freely for the benefit of the developed countries. Moreover, we are one of the topmost buyers of all foreign expensive equipment at exorbitant prices. Also, we are the best in providing wonderful and plentiful opportunities to the foreigners to get associated with the constantly prevalent pathetic conditions on mass scale in our country – poverty, squalor, crime, child labour, etc. – and help the foreigners (and Indians too) win prizes (Nobel, Oscar, etc.) because of the association.

But the fact is that corruption, poverty, hunger, crime, black money and tax evasion are just symptoms of some of the deep-rooted problems. We should attack the root cause of the real problem. The real problem is the total apathy of many of our elected representatives since independence towards the very low living-standard of most of our population and their total incompetence of visionary planning for the progress of nation and its citizens. In this regard, we are at the topmost of the countries having many apathetic, selfish, incompetent elected representatives for about 70 years. Some selfish elected representatives have kept the majority of population deprived and suppressed whereby the majority is forced to live in very difficult and mostly miserable conditions and a few live in extravagantly luxurious conditions. As a result of the selfish interests of some of these representatives, India is suffering from an 'All Wealth and Talent Drain System' (see chapter 2. Analysis) which is working successfully to deprive the population of the results of its hard work as it drains out all the resulting benefits of their hard work to the developed world. India is full of natural resources as well as of talented human resources. Both of these are being utilized very successfully for the betterment and improvement of the lives of the people living in developed countries.

India with its 120 crore population, about 30 lakh sq. km area, many religions, languages, customs, extremely contrasting living standards of different social layers of the society and huge number of problems needs highly competent, public-oriented, empathetic management professionals as elected representatives to manage the country in order to lead it in a direction where all the 100 per cent of the population benefits by the development which should be balanced. We need to reverse the 'All Wealth and Talent Drain System' by a unique transformation program so that the results of the hard-work are returned to the public and the living-standard of all the Indians living in India is made much better (by about 100 times) than now. The population deserves to get the world's best facilities in all the areas – housing, education, transport, health, sports, entertainment, security, infrastructure, employment, etc. If the available natural and human resources are used properly for the benefit of the population, the living standard of people can be made about 100 times better than now in a very short time by providing them the top class facilities, but this has not been/is not being done with the clear intention of keeping the majority of population deprived and suppressed whereby the majority suffers in misery and a few enjoy the life in luxury.

In spite of some significant growth and development in a few sectors, India is currently lagging very much behind compared to the developed countries because of unbalanced development. This is reflected truly in India's current position in the UN Human Development Index which is 135 now in the list of about 190 countries.

India's position can be changed from the current 135 to be in the first 10 within a very short time by implementing an advanced, comprehensive, integrated, powerful, extraordinary, progressive, innovative, drastic, complete, hence Unique Transformation Program. By this unique program, India can be completely transformed into a really developed country similar to any developed West European country within the time limits specified in the program.

The Unique Transformation Program is an integrated program of about 100 huge projects and solutions covering all the domains – agriculture, crime, culture, defense, education, employment, energy, entertainment, environment, health, infrastructure, justice, medicine, nutrition, sanitation, security, sports, technology, transport, etc. and it offers complete solutions for total eradication of corruption, crime, black money, poverty, hunger, unemployment, non-education, tax evasion, malnutrition, exploitation, farmer suicide, heavy price rise, etc.

Some interesting facts to be considered are the following:

1. **Incredible INDIA** is truly **incredible** as it has huge disparities and extreme contrasts found nowhere else. Here, very few people are super rich, and the masses living in miserable conditions are undernourished. India is SHINING only for 5 to 10 per cent and is **NOT** SHINING for 90–95 per cent of the Indian population.

   Huge disparities exist in India – disparities between the top incomes and the lowest, best education for a few and no education for a majority, very high living standards for a handful of people and majority living in either no comfort or filthy conditions.
2. Majority of Indians are the hardest working people and unfortunately, live with the least comforts and the lowest living standard, although there is no dearth of resources, both natural and human resources.

   Khalil Gibran, poet and philosopher from Lebenon, whose name many Indians would not have even heard of, in the same way as many Indians would not have read Gitanjali of Rabindra Nath Tagore, because our priorities about material life have made us so selfish and to some extent even cruel, that we are too busy in our work to earn as much money as possible in the shortest possible time, and sometimes by any means possible, that although India is considered all over the world the only center and source of spiritual knowledge, we, Indians, ignore this fact and forget to read or remember what Tagore said or what Gibran said, says "When you work, you fulfil a part of earth's furthest dream, assigned to you when that dream was born. And in keeping yourself with labour you are in truth loving life, And to love life through labour is to be intimate with life's inmost secret". His saying is nowhere more true than in India because Indians have immense desire to work. They leave their homes, villages, cities, even country in search of work, and they work hard to improve their living conditions.

But unfortunately, as compared to the developed countries where people work less and have all the possible facilities to make the life most comfortable, Indians work the hardest in very difficult conditions, and majority of them live in miserable conditions with the least comforts and the lowest living standard.

In earlier days, the British exported Indians in masses to various countries to work as manual labourers in the sugarcane fields or elsewhere. Nowadays, the work has evolved, and all the work which is done by qualified IT professionals – programmers, analysts, project managers, call center operators, etc., can be grouped as IT labour. The developed countries need cheap IT labour in great quantity and now, that is being provided in bulk by India.

It is already very late but still, better late than never, so it is the right time to decide by Indians whether they want to remain a cheap labour source of both manual labour and IT labour, themselves and their coming generations, and thus remain at the mercy of those who use this cheap labour, be it a handful of Indians or many foreigners. Or, they want to change it all to control their own destiny by themselves, by raising their level of competence in such a manner that they are respected for their innovative skills, a level of competence which when achieved would not be a level of competence used and exploited by the rich people, both Indians and foreigners, in India and in rich/developed countries because of low cost and very low salaries, but which would make the Indians automatically superior, valuable and respected by all the world because of their innovative advanced technical leadership, skills and products.

3. India is suffering from All Drain, not only Brain Drain. Very high quality professional education is provided to a few selected young men and women at the cost of majority of illiterate and extremely poor population. Many of the professionals leave India in search of their better future. Hence, the money of the population, and the educated professionals themselves, are a double loss for India. Then, India buys all the high-tech equipment developed by the Indians working abroad for the companies in the foreign

countries, at exorbitant prices, since there is no indigenous research and development for high-tech equipment. This is a triple loss. Hence, All Drain.

4. Most of the real issues facing India and the people are neither being addressed nor being tackled properly. One of the topmost real issue is the living standard of the majority of Indians living in India and their quality of life. This needs to be improved drastically. The current position of India in the UN Human Development Index which indicates the living standard and quality of life of the population is very low. Indians deserve to have a much better life standard and excellent quality of life.
5. Population is not the real problem at present because India is a huge country, almost a sub-continent, and so, the population density of India is almost equal to the population density of many advanced countries, and population density of many advanced countries is even much more than that of India. Just two examples: India has the same population density as Belgium, one of the developed West European country. Also, Singapore, which in many respects is even better than many European countries, has about 20 times more population density than India.
6. Extreme centralization and huge disparities exist in Indian environment which need to be removed.
7. For developed countries, India is a huge market and cheap labour force for both manual and IT work. At present, the rich and developed countries of the world see India as a huge market for their products and as their very cheap labour source, both IT and non-IT labour. It will be their delightful pleasure if it continues to be so for the next 100 years and 100 years after that and so on. If the current situation in India is not changed, only 5 per cent of the Indians who are already super rich will get all the benefit of the hard work of the remaining 95 per cent and will become mega rich, while the 95 per cent hard-working population will continue to remain deprived of the benefit of its hard-work, and at the same time, the rich and developed countries will benefit the most.

8. Only the Unique Transformation Program will deliver the benefit of hard work of Indians to all the 100 per cent of Indians by raising their living standard drastically, because it will create guaranteed employment for all the Indians in India at different levels automatically for the next at least 100 years, remove the existing huge disparities, and will make India an exporter of all high-tech equipment rather than a cheap labour source for IT and non-IT work of rich and developed countries while remaining an importer of all sorts of equipment and machines.
9. India will become a gigantic superpower and all the Indians will enjoy the benefits of their hard-work only with the Unique Transform ation Program, not by being a cheap labour source of both IT and non-IT labour, nor by importing the foreign made high-tech/heavy/household/consumer/ other equipment/machines, nor with the mercy of any other country, nor by providing cheap manufacturing facilities by cheap labour to the developed foreign countries through 'make in India' type programmes, nor by becoming the cheap back-office of the world because of cheap IT labour, because all these latter steps which are opposite to what is needed as discussed in the unique transformation program in further chapters will never improve the living standard of majority of Indians as the majority of them will remain lowly paid throughout their lives by these measures.

2

Analysis

India's successful All Wealth and Talent Drain system

India is suffering from an All Wealth and Talent Drain system which is working successfully to deprive the population of the results of its hard work as it drains out all the resulting benefits of their hard work to the developed world.

India is full of natural resources as well as of talented human resources. Both of these are being very successfully utilized for the betterment and improvement of the lives of the people living in developed countries.

Following are the facts to show how the developed countries benefit from the hard work of Indians and how Indians are deprived of what they deserve, that is, a much better living standard with the best facilities in all the domains of life – education, medical, health, nutrition, transport, security, sports, culture, entertainment, environment, etc.

1. Every year, India exports the following at very cheap rates:

   a. Mineral ores
   b. Fruits, spices, dry fruits
   c. Clothes made by low-paid workers
   d. Diamonds worked on by low-paid workers
   e. Other export items prepared/worked by low-paid workers
   f. Animal meat (India is one of the biggest meat exporter of the world!)

Exporting national resources at a cheap rate is losing the nation's wealth and exporting articles made by low-paid workers keeps the living standard of the working people very low as they are paid low amounts.

2. Low-priced and very high standard education is given to a selected few at the cost of lowly paid building workers, road making workers, workers in the educational institutions, teachers, farmers, household help workers, etc. The approximate cost of making an engineer in Europe will be about six crore rupees. Many of the engineers and doctors leave India to live and work in developed countries which get readymade engineers and doctors at no cost. Hence, the developed countries not only save their money which they would have to spend to make an engineer/doctor, but they gain doubly as they get engineers/doctors freely from India. If 50 lakh educated Indians have left to work and settle in foreign countries in the past about 50 years, it is worth 300 lakh crore (three thousand kharab) of rupees. So, all the money spent on highly educated citizens is lost for India and is used for the benefit of developed countries. Of course, the educated/trained engineers/doctors are lost naturally.
3. Low-skilled workers leave India to work in Singapore and Middle-East/African countries which are rich. These vulnerable workers are paid very low in contradiction to the rich countries national standards, and they work very hard in difficult situations to build and maintain the high living standard of those countries for their citizens.
   The hard-work of low-paid Indian workers results in the improvement of life of people in the foreign countries.
4. In the past few years, cheap software/IT services are offered by Indian companies to developed countries. The building/infrastructure workers to build the nice buildings and roads for these companies in India are very low paid workers. The Indian companies earn huge profits with the hard-work of their employees and then buy companies in developed countries.
   All the money of the low-paid workers is utilized for the betterment of life of foreigners in two ways, firstly by

providing them cheap services with low-cost workers and secondly, by helping the economies of the foreign countries where the Indian companies buy the foreign companies as the bought-over companies provide employment to the local people there.

5. Big Indian companies employ cheap workers to work in their companies like tea fields, etc. The conditions of these workers have remained the same during the last 50 years because they are as lowly paid today as about 50 years ago, but the company owners of these companies buy big companies in various sectors such as steel, cars, etc. in developed countries.

   The profits earned as a result of the hard-work of low-paid workers are utilized for the benefit of the foreign workers in the foreign companies located abroad that are bought by the Indian owners.

6. Huge amount of black money earned through unfair means by some corrupt citizens gets deposited in the Swiss or other countries' banks where it is used for investments in developed countries for the benefit of the population there. So, the hard-earned money of Indians given as bribes to corrupt Indian people is used to finance the economic activities in the developed world improving their conditions still further.

7. Developed countries use the cheap mineral ores imported from India to produce big and sophisticated equipment with the help of freely supplied engineers from India, and India buys these equipment at exorbitant prices.

   So, India loses in four ways, firstly, by selling the raw mineral resources cheaply, secondly, spending poor people's money to make engineers and losing that money as engineers leave to work abroad, and then, supplying those well-educated/trained engineers free of cost, and last but not the least, buying very expensive equipment made from the cheaply sold Indian natural resources and made by the freely supplied Indian human resources.

8. Multi-national companies employ cheaply available engineers, workers in their companies in India and earn huge profits because of cheap Indian labour.

All the profit earned by these companies due to the hard-work of Indian workers goes to the share-holders and governments/citizens of the developed countries.

To summarise, developed countries benefit from the money of the Indian hard workers who don't get this money which they deserve by the following ways:

A. By investing in industries and infrastructure the money which came from India through corruption,
B. By utilizing Indian money in foreign companies which have been bought over by Indian owners in developed countries by the wealth the Indian owners amassed in their Indian companies by paying very low wages to hard working Indians,
C. By saving the money through
   a. buying cheap raw mineral resources from India,
   b. importing from India free highly qualified and experienced professionals who received high quality education very cheaply at the cost of low-paid workers in India, and
   c. importing cheap low educated workers from India.
D. By getting cheap services from Indian companies which pay low wages to their workers in India,
E. By earning huge profits through selling at exorbitant prices to India the products made by
   a. either freely received Indian professionals,
   b. or low cost professionals received from cheap Indian service companies,
   c. or low cost professionals employed in India by foreign companies established in India.

This shows how India's All Wealth and Talent Drain system is working so efficiently that the majority of its own population, with a very low standard of life, suffers from poverty and hunger while the benefits of the hard work of Indians go to the developed countries. All the drain ensures that all the good facilities in India are scarce and they are available to only a few Indians. The result is that India's place

- in the UN Human Development Index List 2014 is 135 in the list of about 190 countries (the higher the number in the list, the worse),
- in the Global Hunger Index 2014 is 55 in the list of 76 worst ranked countries from about 200 countries of the world (the higher the number in the list, the worse),
- in the Environmental Performance Index 2014 is 155 out of 178 countries (the higher the number in the list, the worse),
- in the Corruption Perception Index 2013 is 94 in 177 countries (the higher the number in the list, the worse),
- in the infant mortality rate 2012 list is 50 in a list of 221 countries (the lower the number in the list, the worse),
- in the Global Peace index 2014 is 144 in a list of 157 countries (the higher the number in the list, the worse),
- is number one in the World Health Organisation/UNICEF 2012 list of people not having toilets and defecating in open – 63 crore Indians (the lower the number in the list, the worse).

On the other hand, all the citizens of the developed countries enjoy excellent life because Indians are working for the betterment and maintenance of their high living-standards in developed countries.

We need to reverse the All Wealth and Talent Drain system by the unique transformation program so that the results of the hard-work are returned to the public and the living-standard of all the Indians living in India is made much better than now.

3

Vision

Vision

The following statement can seem a very simplistic view, but it is in fact very effective. If all the problems prevailing in India are combined together to make the essence of problems as one problem and then, provide the solution to that one problem, all the problems can be solved simultaneously. In India, that one problem which can also be measured is the living standard of majority of Indians and it is measured by the position in the UN Human Development Index which in the case of India currently is 135 in the list of about 190 countries. So, the vision is to raise the living standard of the majority of the population in order to improve drastically the position of India in the UN Human Development Index. Hence:

The *VISION* is to raise the living standard of 100 percent of the Indian population by about 100 times to move India in the top ten of the UN Human Development Index from the current 135th position within about five to eight years that will be achieved by the advanced, comprehensive, integrated, powerful, extraordinary, progressive, innovative, drastic, complete, hence Unique Transformation Programme.

4

Values

Values

The transformation programme supports and promotes the following values at every level of the nation including all the states, cities and villages, for all the people of India living everywhere in India.

True democracy

The programme supports and promotes the power of the people and power by the people. People decide what is best for them. People monitor and direct the working of the elected representative in regular weekly meetings with them on Saturdays and Sundays.

Equality

The programme supports and promotes the balanced development throughout the country for the benefit of all the 100 per cent of the population without any consideration of cast or religion.

Accountability

The programme supports and promotes the accountability. Elected representatives are accountable to the public. They represent the public to serve the public, they are not rulers (they are "maali" in Hindi, not "maalik" in Hindi). So the public is the master, the elected representatives have to follow the directions from the public and hence are accountable to the public.

Respect and sympathy

The programme supports and promotes the respect for all the citizens and is sympathetic to the citizens of the deprived sections of the society. It will improve drastically the living conditions of all the citizens, especially of all the people in 70 per cent lower income groups.

Innovation

The program believes in innovative methods to improve the conditions of all the population. It will change all the outdated and obsolete methods with much better methods to implement the transformation program for the benefit of all the population.

Excellence

The program supports and promotes excellence and will provide all the best and excellent facilities of the world to all the 100 per cent population all over the country.

5

Characteristics

Unique Transformation Programme Characteristics

The unique transformation programme has the following characteristics:

1. It is advanced, comprehensive, integrated, powerful, extraordinary, progressive, innovative, drastic, complete, hence unique in nature.
2. If implemented carefully and correctly, the transformation program will create about 13 crore jobs in India in the next two to five years.
3. It will make India the ultimate real and moral power on earth by raising the living standard of 100 per cent of the Indian population by about 100 times to make India's place in the first ten of the UN Human Development Index from the current 135 within five to eight years ensuring real equal status for all the citizens.
4. It is comprehensive, complete and well-structured for balanced, organized and sustainable development.
5. It offers complete solutions for total eradication of corruption, crime, black money, poverty, hunger, unemployment, non-education, tax evasion, malnutrition, exploitation, farmer suicide, heavy price rise, etc.
6. It covers all the domains – agriculture, crime, culture, defense, education, employment, energy, entertainment, environment,

health, infrastructure, justice, medicine, nutrition, sanitation, security, sports, technology, transport, etc.

7. Everything in the programme is for the benefit and welfare of all the citizens regardless of their background, education, religion, caste, etc.
8. It will provide all the best facilities to all the 100 per cent population at all the places in India in all the domains.
9. It is designed with special attention for the 70 per cent lower income group, economically weaker sections, women, farmers, children and rural areas.
10. It provides all the benefits of the planned balanced development to all the 100 per cent population living all over the country.
11. There are many excellent features in the program, for example, regarding health, black-money, tax-evasion, crime, etc. which are not available in even the developed West European countries.
12. It is based on already realized, implemented and well-established model of the highly-advanced, developed West European countries, includes in many respects several improved features over and above this, and is very realistic.
13. It applies business process improvement/re-engineering for most of the national processes.
14. It takes care of sustained development by top class research, development, manufacturing facilities.
15. It incorporates best governance by strict discipline/ monitoring.
16. It aims to emulate the best:

    We should not be shy to absorb and practice the best features from other countries while maintaining our own traditional/ cultural/family values, for example, the best

    - educational/technological and other facilities in USA/ West Europe
    - governance/organization/cleanliness in Singapore
    - socialistic welfare pattern in West Europe
    - nationalistic spirit for self-dependence in high-tech areas in China

- equal, very fast justice to all in the USA
- high-quality products/equipment in Germany and Japan

17. There is nothing in the program which is impossible to achieve. Everything in the program is 100 per cent possible to achieve.
18. Training

Many of the elected representatives in India are not management professionals. They lack management skills and leadership qualities. As a result, there is a lot of mismanagement, poor management and absence of management in India leading to highly unbalanced growth/development. India, with its highly complex environment and requirements, desperately needs well-trained political leaders who can manage professionally a balanced development in India.

To implement the unique transformation program, an intensive, advanced political leadership programme especially suited for Indian environment and conditions within the context of the current global situation is required. This "Advanced Political Leadership Intensive Program" is highly suitable for the needs of all the political leaders in India. It will train the Indian political leaders to teach them how effective the leaders should be, what great work in what systematically organized, planned manner, and how efficiently they should do.

As mentioned earlier, India's position in the UN Human Development Index can be changed from the current 135 to be in the first ten within a very short time by implementing the unique transformation programme for India. By this unique transformation programme, India can be completely transformed into a really developed country to become similar to any developed West European country within the time limits specified in the programme.

To implement the unique transformation programme, the political leaders in India who either are or aspire to become elected representatives need to be trained to make them understand about the details and importance of the transformation programme and to prepare them for their effective leadership role in its implementation.

The core contents of the Advanced Political Intensive Leadership programme are:

a. Political issues related to India;
b. The unique transformation programme for India to raise the living standard of about 120 crore Indian citizens by about 100 times within about 5 to 8 years;
c. The implementation strategy of this transformation programme.

The above content items can be presented as follows:

a. Political issues:

- Analysis;
- Vision;
- Values;
- People characteristics;
- Basic policies;

b. Transformation plan:

- Characteristics;
- Top priority areas;
- Primary national goals;
- Ultimate national goals;
- Implementation strategy details;
- Basic strategic outline;
- List of major projects;
- Strategic implementation model/formulae;
- Main systems, sub-systems and programs;
- Tasks lists.

6

Top Priority Areas

Unique Transformation Programme's Top Priority Areas

The top priority areas of the unique transformation programme for all the population living all over the country are the following:

A. Basic life requirements

Sanitary and high-standard living conditions

1. Housing – modern, comfortable housing with 24-hours water, electricity and gas; toilet, and road connection for all
2. Hygiene and cleanliness – garbage management, public toilets provision and pollution-free environment
3. Poverty and hunger – zero poverty and zero hunger by raising the living standard of all the population especially the 75 per cent lower income group and by providing education with full employment opportunities; high-quality, cheap supermarkets and public restaurants for all the public
4. Price control – cheap and affordable prices for food, daily use items, education, transport, petrol, gas, etc.
5. Extremely low (nearly zero) inflation
6. Equality, full justice and the best facilities in all the domains for all the citizens living all over the country irrespective of caste and religion.

7. Rural development – all the best facilities for education, health, sports, agriculture, entertainment, employment, security, culture, transport, roads, etc. in villages and small/medium cities; decentralization from big cities towards other parts
8. Child malnutrition – special help and attention for children and mothers
9. Food adulteration – zero. It will be completely stopped by strict rules, checks and severe punishments
10. Health care – top class very cheap health care for all; complete eradication of tuberculosis, malaria, asthma, leprosy; free health check by doctor home visit for above 55 (not even in Europe)
11. Child labour – complete stop
12. Top class sports and cultural facilities

B. Life sustaining and maintaining requirements

1. Employment – full employment for all through education, industries and research centers for new, innovative and high technology products by accelerating the economic growth rate from existing 8-10 per cent to 16-20 per cent
2. Education – zero illiteracy through top class very cheap primary, secondary, professional education for all, special attention for girls; only arts, music, dance, sports, yoga till 6 years; no entry exam for any higher education only exit exams; change of exam system – to be application oriented not memorization; large number of libraries and reading-rooms
3. Corruption-free governance – zero corruption; Lokpal and Lokayukts; simple rules, strict monitoring/control and quick action for absolute transparency and corruption-free governance
4. Zero black money and zero tax evasion
5. Farmer suicide – zero farmer suicide with special attention to the needs of farmers and agriculture sector
6. Agricultural reforms – labour, storage, product sale, irrigation, marketing hubs, road connection, seeds/organic fertilizers outlets, loans, etc.

7. Political/elections reforms – RTI, election process, all above 18 year voting properly
8. Tax Reforms – rationalization of all the taxes for the benefit of lower and middle income groups
9. Highly improved judicial system
10. Improved industrial policies to promote business environment
11. Control on drugs, vulgarity, obscenity in public
12. Strict pollution control

C. Comfortable life requirements

1. Transport – top class cheap multiple transport facilities with high quality transport infrastructure for all
2. Increase in buying power of the lowest 80 per cent income holders
3. Social security, pension, medical insurance for all

D. Safe life requirements

1. Crime-free living – zero crime with complete safety of all the citizens, especially women/girls everywhere
2. Robust and sound national security through radically improved armed forces of army, navy and air-force
3. Flood/drought control for zero death by flood/drought
4. Disaster recovery centers
5. Communal harmony
6. Citizen's complaints centers
7. Help centers for all kind of problems

E. Life entertainment requirements

1. Tourism promotion
2. Fun/entertainment parks

7

Primary Goals

Unique Transformation Programme's Primary Goals

The Primary goals of the unique transformation program for all the population living all over the country are the following:

The requirements of all the population of the whole nation are considered to provide the best facilities, administration, infrastructure, etc. to all the citizens regardless of their religion, caste, etc.

1. Complete eradication of corruption, poverty, hunger, malnutrition, crime, black money, tax evasion, non-education, unemployment, farmer suicide, exploitation, heavy price rise, food adulteration; Lokpal and Lokayukts; simple rules, strict monitoring/control and quick action for absolute transparency and corruption-free governance
2. Equality, full justice and the best facilities in all the domains for all the citizens living all over the country irrespective of caste and religion.
3. Strict price control with extremely low (nearly zero) inflation
4. Rural development – all the best facilities for education, health, sports, agriculture, entertainment, employment, security, culture, transport, roads, etc. in villages and

small/medium cities, decentralization from big cities towards other parts

5. Child malnutrition – special help and attention for children and mothers
6. Child labour – complete stop
7. Very high standard cheap high/medium/low level education facilities for all the children and adults; special attention for girls; 100 per cent education (and not literacy) for all the citizens by making education up to 12th class a fundamental right of every citizen; salary of teachers at par with international standards, public libraries and reading-rooms.
8. Full employment through education, industries and research centers for new, innovative and high technology products by accelerating the economic growth rate from existing 8-10 per cent to 16-20 per cent; Promotion of economically backward people in jobs and education irrespective of their caste, religion or sex
9. Top class very cheap health care through fully equipped high standard hospitals for all the population; complete eradication of tuberculosis, malaria, asthma, leprosy; free health check by doctor home visit for above 55 (not even in Europe); autonomous medical commission for ensuring good standard of doctors and to check medical mal-practice; special benefits for doctors working in rural areas
10. Agricultural reforms – labour, storage, product sale, irrigation, marketing hubs, road connection, seeds/organic fertilisers outlets, loans; Immediate attention to prevent farmer's suicides in various parts of our country; full crop insurance
11. Modern, comfortable housing with 24-hours water, electricity gas, toilet and road connection for all
12. Hygiene and cleanliness – garbage management and public toilets provision
13. Internal security – at least three to five well-trained, well-equipped, well-paid citizen friendly police persons for every 100 citizens; police independent from politicians for transfers
14. Drastically improved armed forces of army, navy and air-force in number and modern advanced weapon systems/ equipment

15. Transport – top class cheap multiple transport facilities with high quality transport infrastructure for all
16. Increase in buying power of the lowest 80 per cent income holders
17. Social security, pension, medical insurance for all
18. Political/elections reforms – RTI, election process, all above 18 years voting properly
19. Pollution free environment
20. Top quality all sports facilities for all the population
21. Varied entertainment facilities for all and tourism promotion – high-quality cheap hotels
22. Extreme cleanliness of roads and all the public places
23. Varied cultural activities
24. Citizen friendly administration for quick birth/marriage/ death registration/certificates, passport, etc.
25. Complete safety of all the population especially for women
26. Quick justice availability
27. Best working conditions for all the workers in all the sectors
28. Basic amenities availability for all the population – water, electricity, gas, etc.
29. Very good shopping facilities for all the population
30. Industries for all the products to make the imports of all the modern high-tech equipment zero and to export all the products
31. Citizens complaints centers for quick actions
32. Strict traffic control
33. Communal harmony promotion by building worship centers for all the communities – temples/mosques/churches/ gurudwaras – in single compounds
34. Intensive national integration - promotion of nationalism and breaking of regionalism
35. Improved industrial policies to promote business environment – special incentives/awards for entrepreneurs; free of bureaucracy
36. High-quality, cheap supermarkets and public restaurants for all the public
37. All the best facilities/arrangements for all the population all over the country in all the areas – education, health, transport, sports, employment, energy, technology, agriculture, defense, nutrition, security, culture, entertainment, environment, etc.

38. Setting-up Help Centers for all kind of problems especially for farmers, women, emergency, crime, etc.
39. Control on drugs, vulgarity, obscenity in public
40. Professional migration compensation from the immigration country

8

Unique Transformation Programme Summary with Time-line

Unique Transformation Programme Summary

Ultimate Top Goal: to raise the living standard of 100 per cent of the Indian population by about 100 times to move India in TOP 10 of the UN Human Development Index List from the current 135th position.

A. UNIQUE PROGRAMMMME'S EXTRAORDINARY ULTIMATE GOALS (all 100 per cent possible to achieve) for DRASTIC IMPROVEMNT IN THE LIVING STANDARD OF ALL, i.e., 100 times better quality of life of all the Indians living in India that all the Indian population deserves and needs:

1. Zero corruption in India, to become No. 1 in the list of non-corrupt countries – 2 months
2. Zero black money, zero tax evasion – 2 years
3. 10 crore new jobs – 2 years
4. Comfortable, modern housing for all 100 per cent of the population with road and 24 hours electricity, water, gas connection, and toilets – 8 years

5. 10 times increase in buying power of the lowest 80 per cent income holders – 8 years
6. Extremely low (nearly zero) inflation – 2 years
7. 200 Olympic Gold medals, world top 100 tennis, badminton, table tennis players each, no.1 hockey, football, athletics, ski, volleyball, basketball, swimming teams each – 8 years
8. 10 Nobel prizes – 8 years
9. Average age increase by 20 years of all the population, and average height increase by 10 cms of the shortest 90 per cent of the population – 8 years
10. Automatic massive flood/drought control system (canal/reservoir/pumping network) and weather (fog/rain/storm/humidity) control system – 8 years
11. Public transport system 100 times better and extensive road, rail, air-travel network, strict road traffic control rules – 4 years
12. Social security, pension, medical insurance for all, free health check by doctor home visit for above 55 (not even in Europe) – 2 years
13. Internal/external security, police, army, navy, air-force proportional to population and size of India, 10 to 50 times more – 2 years
14. Education reforms, children 3 – 6 years arts, yoga, languages (regional, foreign), sports, 100 per cent literacy, professional education, Indian/foreign languages, all education of very high standard and free – 3 years
15. Tax reforms, to use the citizen's money for the benefit of all the citizens themselves, not for the benefit of super-rich countries – 3 years
16. Saturdays, Sundays public meetings of elected representatives with public all over India, monitoring, suggestions, directions by citizens, immediate action, so that the citizens become more participants and less spectators – 3 months
17. Political system reforms, Lok, Vidhan, Rajyasabha, governor, etc., so that the public money is not wasted – 2 years
18. Cleanliness, hygiene 100 times better, 2 lakh rose/other flowers gardens – 2 years

19. Immediate help in disaster like flood, earthquake, etc., no deaths due to floods, summer heat or cold in winter – 2 years
20. Zero crime and 100 times faster justice system – 3 years
21. 100 times better solution for reservation policy leading to abolition of reservation – 2 years
22. Strict control of noise, industrial, emission, other pollution, 100 times reduction in pollution, no night flight landing/ take-off – 4 years
23. Research centers for energy, information and communication technology, health and pharmaceutical, aeronautics, transport, bio-technology, defense, intelligent systems, heavy machines, semiconductor and security – 3 years
24. 10 thousand fun/entertainment parks – 4 years
25. Agriculture output 20 times more – 4 years
26. Zero food adulteration – 1 year
27. Zero child labour – 1 year
28. Zero poverty – 4 years
29. Withdrawal from the ex-slaves club (commonwealth) – 3 months
30. Indian rupee the topmost currency of the world – 8 years
31. Special help centers for farmers, women, emergency, crime, availability of doctors/chemists on weekends/holidays/nights – 1 year
32. Wildlife protection and tourism promotion for foreigners/ Indians – 3 years
33. Control on drugs, vulgarity, obscenity in public – 1 year

B. SOLUTIONS/HUGE PROJECTS TO ACHIEVE THE GOALS (all 100 per cent possible by the formulae, processes, techniques, strategy and solutions based on already available, well-implemented, proven models) and 50 times INDIAN RUPEE VALUE INCREASE, by all the following own Indian R&D, design and manufacturing facilities:

1. L44 fighter plane (2xF22), helicopter, submarine, tank, missile, warship, aircraft carrier, radar, all defense

equipment more advanced than the current best technology – 8 years

2. 500 seats, 3000Km/hour airplane, 600 airports, 30 international airports at least one in each state – 8 years
3. 600km/hour fast trains, 5 hours journey from Kashmir to Kanyakumari, 5 hours from Amritsar to Imphal, completely transformed advanced rail system with modern infrastructure – 8 years
4. Manned exploration/space lab for other solar systems, intermediate destination Mars – 12 years
5. 50 per cent solar, 50 per cent nuclear fusion and other renewable energy, 100 nuclear reactors – 8 years
6. Telecom research, own telecom equipment, all households optical connection – 4 years
7. Indian PC, supercomputer – 4 years
8. 200 IIT's, 200 AIIMS's, 200 IIM's, 60 thousand medium/low-skill (technical/non-technical) professional schools, 1.8 lakh public libraries and reading-rooms – 4 years
9. One lakh sport clubs with sport courts, athletic and gymnastic facilities for all the children, young and old persons, 60 thousand swimming pools, one lakh fitness centers, 20 thousand top sport schools – two years
10. 60 thousand top class hospitals – 4 years
11. Innovative product development, cyclone prevention, weather control, future travel, etc. – 8 years
12. Indian luxury car, comfortable bus – 8 years
13. World's biggest land/space telescope – 8 years
14. Micro/nano-chips development – 4 years
15. All latest medical instruments, more advanced than the current best technology – 4 years
16. All heavy industrial machines, road building machines, cranes, CNC, others – 8 years
17. All consumer electronics, home appliances – 8 years
18. Filth and environment management, 3 persons per sq. km for maintaining cleanliness – 2 years
19. 60 thousand well-equipped disaster help/recovery centres – 2 years

20. 50 times increase in judicial system infrastructure, courts, judges, staff, etc. – 3 years
21. New social department linked with tax, employment, education, internal security, housing departments, 60 thousand Managed Zones with 13 responsibilities each, all connected through mobile video-VPN – 1 year
22. 60 thousand music schools, Indian classic (Indian instruments, south, north, Rabindra sangeet)/Western classic (piano, violin, cello, oboe, mandolin, orchestra), 60 thousand art schools, 1.2 lakh auditoriums – 2 years
23. 20 lakh extremely clean and hygienic public toilets, out of which one lakh each in 10 big cities – 2 years
24. Agricultural research and reforms, better, advanced farming techniques, subsidies, financial help for farmers – 3 years
25. 60 thousand cheap, big, high-quality supermarkets to keep prices under control and 10 thousand modern milk dairies – 3 years
26. On-line payment network for zero black money, zero tax-evasion with 30 lakh on-line payment service centers and three lakh bank branches with compulsory bank account for all individuals, business; payment only by bank transfer/card; maximum money withdrawal Rs 1,000 per month for all – 2 years
27. 60 thousand high quality, cheap, clean and hygienic public restaurants – 1 year
28. New technology-oriented suitable cross-discipline engineering education – 2 years
29. 30 thousand top quality hotels, 30 to 50 times more foreign tourists – 2 years
30. Professional migration compensation from the immigration country – 2 years

All the above is 100 per cent possible by replacing the outdated, obsolete, old working methods, techniques and processes with the new, modern, well-proven, special, professional, innovative techniques, processes and methods described further.

Time Plan

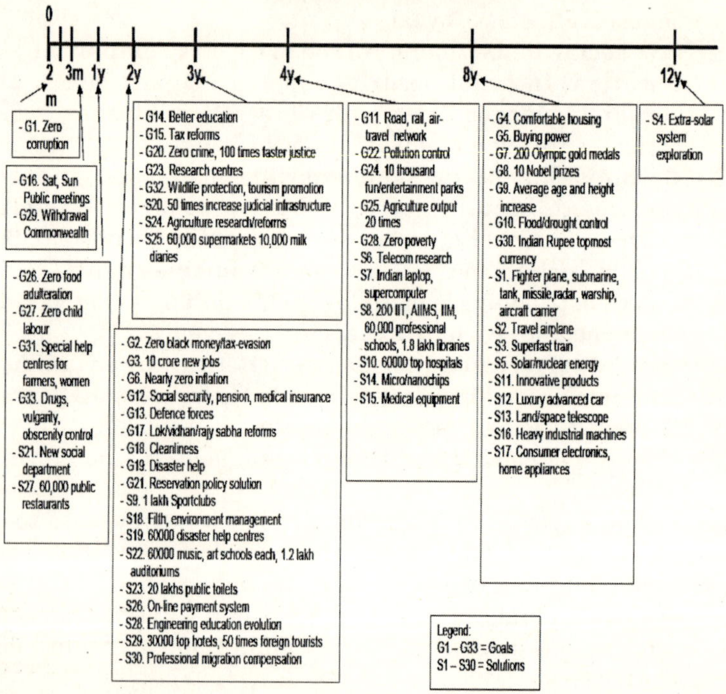

Implementation of the above programme will make India the topmost country in the world.

Efforts to improve the conditions should continue to make the conditions such that in India there is not even a single

- person who has to beg, or is shelter-less or remains hungry due to poverty
- farmer who is forced to commit suicide
- woman/girl who is raped and is not safe
- boy or girl who commits suicide because of failure or scare of failure in studies
- person forced to live in inhumane conditions.

9

Unique Transformation Programme's Ultimate Top Goal

Ultimate Top Goal:

To raise the living standard of 100 per cent of the population by about 100 times to move India in the top 10 of the UN Human Development Index from the current 135th position.

Balanced development based on a well-structured, well-planned, well-organised, well-controlled transformation programme can be achieved very easily to raise the living standard of all the population everywhere in India by providing the best facilities to all in all the domains. Modern Information Systems can be used for the implementation and control of the transformation programme. All the huge disparities and extreme contrasts in our country can be removed and the true result of the hard work of the people can be returned to the people themselves. It is 100 per cent possible to achieve the top goal.

10

Extraordinary Ultimate Goals

Extraordinary Ultimate Goals:

The following extraordinary ultimate goals are formulated to achieve the one ultimate top goal of raising the living standard of all the population to move India in the first 10 of the UN Human Development Index.

Corruption eradication

G1. Zero corruption to become No. 1 in the list of non-corrupt countries – two months

Corruption in India is prevalent and is the root cause of many evils in the society. It is deeply rooted in three layers. The first layer consists of some of the elected representatives who either may be themselves corrupt or if not themselves corrupt, tolerate the corruption by closing their eyes since they are incapable of taking any action against it. The second layer is of some of the top officials and bureaucrats who indulge in corruption by their shameful denial of all moral and ethical values. The third layer is of some of the clerical staff busy making money by exploiting the situation of helpless citizens who fall prey to their greedy and avaricious demands.

All this can be very well changed and corrected. If the top layer is full of honest and sincere people a lot can be achieved.

Enforcement of strict anti-corruption laws can stop corruption at the middle layer. Improvement in all the facilities and buying power can remove corruption of the bottom layer (see other items further for more details).

Economic Growth

G2. Zero black money, zero tax evasion – two years

This can be achieved by drastic reforms in the payment and tax systems (see details in other items below).

Employment Opportunities

G3. 13 crore new jobs – two years

With the Unique Transformation Programme's full implementation, about 13 crore new jobs at various levels will be created all over India in different domains.

Best Living Facilities

G4. Provide decent air-conditioned housing with toilet and 24-hours electricity, water, gas and road connection for all 100 per cent population – eight years

The goal of air-conditioned housing with 24 hours electricity, water and gas connection for all has many hidden goals. Current situation is that the majority of people either don't have a house and they live on streets, or they live in mud houses or in slums made of walls and rooves of polythene sheets. They don't have water, electricity, toilets, etc. Air-conditioned house has an essential pre-requirement that there must be a house, a real brick-cement built house with 24-hours electricity, water, toilet, etc.

So, this one goal provides, first of all, a decent housing for all, and in the next step, makes it possible for all to have 24-hours electricity, water, gas and road connection and finally an a/c house (see other items for details).

Purchasing Power

G5. 10 times increase in purchasing power of the lowest 80 per cent income holders – eight years

The statistics propagated regarding economic growth do not reveal the real facts. Consider the examples below.

Regarding the price and income evolution in the past 40 years:

Some people who were earning 10 crores of rupees are earning thousands or lakhs of crores now. On the other hand, for the majority of people, hardships have increased because of no miraculous increase in their incomes and very high increase in the prices. The prices in the last about 40 years have gone up by about 150 times or more but the incomes of the lower 80 per cent income holders would have increased by about 20 to 50 times only leading to tremendous difficulties for the majority of the people. To correct this, the buying power of the lowest 80 per cent income holders must be increased by at least 10 times.

Regarding statistical data which gives utterly false impressions:

If someone is earning 100 crores of rupees annually and employs 100 people whose salary is 1 lakh rupees, the average salary of these 101 persons is about 1 crore. If at the same place live about 1000 more people who provide services to the 101 people and they earn 3000 rupees per month, the average salary for these 1,101 people is about 10 lakhs. Now, if at the same place live about 10 thousand more people who don't have any job, and their income is zero, the average salary of these 11,101 people is about 1 lakh. So, statistically, it is a very bright picture. About 11 thousand people having an average salary of 1 lakh. But the reality is entirely different. We have to consider the reality and attack at the real problems and handle the real issues.

Purchasing power can be increased by providing employment to all the people and keeping prices under control.

a. Employment can be achieved by making the best facilities for education and training available and by providing abundant employment opportunities with good salaries,
b. Employment opportunities of better paid jobs can be increased by our own home research and development, design and manufacturing facilities,
c. Prices can be kept under control with the help of public supermarkets
(see further details for the above items).

Increasing the Purchasing power of the lowest 80 per cent income holder will result in

a. Eradicating poverty and reducing the gap between the rich and poor,
b. Uplift of financial standards of middle and poor class people,
c. Raising per-capita yearly income to equivalent of 30 thousand US$.

Inflation

G6. Extremely low (nearly zero) inflation – two years

Within the past about 30 to 40 years, prices of essential and all other commodities have increased by about 150 times. This has led to tremendous decrease in the buying power of Rupee and consequently, the value of Indian Rupee has decreased drastically. Control on inflation is very necessary and important to maintain a good value of Indian Rupee's buying power. This can be achieved by the solutions proposed later for price control, own home R&D, design and manufacturing of all the high-tech equipment for own use and for international sale that will stop the import of costly equipment and replace the import by export of our own designed and manufactured equipment thereby increasing national income, so this will start a reverse trend than now which will lead to almost zero inflation.

Sports

G7. Win 200 Olympic Gold medals, world top 100 tennis, badminton, table tennis players each, No.1 hockey, football, athletics, volleyball, basketball, swimming, ski teams each – eight years

Very small countries with about one crore population, that means about 20 lakhs young people, win 20 or 30 gold medals in the Olympic games every time. India has about 50 to 60 crores of children and young men. It is a pity that with such a large resource, we do not get even a single gold medal in Olympic games. This all has to change. We deserve at least 200 Olympic gold medals. We must have world top tennis, badminton, table tennis players each, and also world No. 1 teams for hockey, football, athletics, basketball, volleyball, ski, swimming, etc. each.

This can be achieved by improved health with better nutrition as a result of better buying power, and by providing the best sport facilities (see details in other items).

Talent

G8. Win 10 Nobel prizes – eight years

India, with its large pool of talented people in every field, deserves to get at least 10 Nobel prizes. This can be achieved by providing the best educational facilities, research centers and design/manufacturing facilities (see details in other items). How research can help to get Nobel prizes can be understood by the following example: take a book of first year of medical studies on human physiology of about 1500 pages by any foreign writer (foreign writer because many Indians have tendency to value all that comes from foreigners). On each page, it would be mentioned many times regarding the functioning of many mechanisms in the human body that 'it is believed', 'it is presumed', 'the reason is not known', 'it is not understood', or similar statements, etc. If on an average we take three such statements per page, we have about 4500 cases where research can be done to find out what the reality is. If about 100 top class medical research facilities are set up and about 500 to 1000 top class medical doctors and experts are assigned to do the research on about 50 per cent of these 4500 cases, i.e., on about 2000 topics, it is possible that the real facts for about 50 per cent of the cases, i.e., about 1000 can be found. Out of that, even if we take 10 per cent of the cases worth winning a Nobel prize, that would be 100. For those 100 cases, even if we get Nobel prize for 10 per cent of them, that will be 10 Nobel prizes, that also, only in medical field. Similarly, research in all other fields can bring many more Nobel prizes.

Average Age

G9. Average age increase by 20 years of all the population, and average height increase by 8 cms of the shortest 90 per cent of the population – eight years

There is so much of malnutrition for children, young and old, all over the country and at the same time, there are several types of diseases which are not found anywhere else in the developed world but are still prevalent in India. Life expectancy is very low compared to that in the developed countries. This needs to be changed and improved by 20 years on average. At the same time, average height of Indians needs to be increased drastically.

This can be achieved by providing the best medical, health and sport facilities with drastically improved nutrition, based on increased buying power (see other items for details).

Floods and Droughts

G10. Provide automatic massive flood/drought control system (canal/reservoir/pumping network) and weather (fog/rain/storm/humidity) control system – eight years

Whenever it rains, there are floods in different parts of India, killing mostly the poor people who don't have any solid shelter. Then, there are droughts when there is no rain and the poor suffer again. With so many rivers and so much of rains, there needs to be designed an automatic massive flood/drought control system to utilize the natural gifts in a suitable and useful manner for the welfare of all the citizens.

This can be achieved with planned connection of all the major rivers from north to south and east to west and designing the automated canal/reservoir/pumping network systems.

Similarly, automatic weather control system for controlling fog, rain, storm, humidity can help achieve a much better life than now.

Traffic and Road Network

G11. Provide much better public transport system and extensive road, rail, air-travel network with strict road traffic control rules – four years

We need a top-class public transport system with extensive road network and well-disciplined strict traffic rules, in order to reduce the chaos on poorly maintained roads. Many rich people and middle class people have very good cars. But what is the use of the cars if there are no good roads or no roads at all to drive? The poor quality of the existing roads and the lack of rules make it a nightmare to drive.

For this, all the villages and small towns should be connected by the best roads to the national road network and the best transport facilities – bus, underground train/metro, trains –

should be provided for all the citizens connecting all the villages, towns, schools, hospitals, residential areas, shopping centers, public buildings, etc.

Similarly, we need a modern, advanced, extensive rail network and air-travel network with all the best facilities.

Social Security

G12. Provide social security, pension, medical insurance for all and have free health check by doctor home visit for above 55 (not even in Europe) – two years

All the citizens need a social security system. Those who are employed in good companies or by the government, enjoy some good benefits like medical care, or pension etc. But, those who don't have good jobs or those who work on their own account or those who run small or medium businesses have no guarantee of social security or medical facilities. It all needs to be changed and every citizen, whether employed, unemployed, or having own business must be covered by social security and pension schemes.

This will also provide necessary help to all the needy and medically unfit persons who need special help due to health or fitness, or due to any disability.

Internal and External Security

G13. Ensure internal and external security by making police, army, navy and air-force proportional to population and size of India meaning 10 to 50 times more than now – two years

India is a vast country and needs proper internal and external security arrangements which are not being done properly at present. If our borders are properly guarded, there is no reason that any terrorist can cross from the neighboring lands.

Similarly, if the internal security is taken care of properly, there is no reason that crimes can happen.

We need to build up internal and external security forces according to the population and size of India, which means sufficient number of security forces with all the modern facilities and equipment. In general, about 4 to 5 per cent of the population should be employed and engaged for internal and external security.

Education

G14. Implement education reforms to have 100 per cent literacy, professional education, Indian/foreign languages with all the education of very high standard and free, to have only yoga, arts, languages (regional, foreign) and sports education for 3–6 years old children – three years

The complete education system needs to be drastically reformed.

At present, in primary and kindergarten schools, interviews of 3-years old children's parents are held for children's admission to school. Childrens are loaded with books like donkeys. How many Nobel prizes have we won with all this unnecessary overloading?

At the same time, 50 per cent of children would not have entered a school. That means that 50 per cent of the talent is already lost.

Balanced education needs to be provided to all the children of India. And the education should be such that provides means to allow the full personality growth, to make good humans and citizens, to make possible the utilization of the full potential of individuals.

Some of the required important and necessary features for a top-class education system which needs to be implemented in India are mentioned below:

a. No entrance exam for any field of education in any educational institute/college/university should be there; only strict exit assessment system should be there to award a degree or diploma.
b. Possibility and provision of switching the education direction for the students should be there.
c. Abundance of top class educational institutions for all kinds of higher/medium/lower general/professional education should be there. If there are 10 lakh students who want to study at IIT or AIIMS or IIM every year, there should be 200 IITs, 200 AIIMS and 200 IIMs without any entrance exam. The students who wish to study there should just enroll for the course and join without any entrance test. Proper guiding facilities for the students should be provided to ascertain the aptitude before selecting a particular

direction and admission to particular courses. Students should select the directions and courses based on their interests, abilities and the guidance received. There should be strict exam system during and after the course to allow only the right students to continue and go ahead. For the remaining unsuitable students, it should be possible to switch to other less demanding study directions with suitable guidance from the guiding facilities.

d. Assessment by judging the abilities and capacity of understanding, analyzing, applying and using the course matter should be there, not by memorizing. So, the exam system should be changed. Exam should be conducted to judge the ability to analyze and apply the knowledge, not only memorization ability.
e. All primary education should be uniform, controlled by state: special attention for character building, and only art, languages, music, yoga, sports till 6 years of age should be there.
f. Financial help for financially weak families' children should be provided.
g. Lessons help for students who are weak in studies should be provided.
h. Compulsory education for children till graduation or technical/professional education should be there.

Income Tax

G15. Tax reforms, to use the citizens' money for the benefit of all the citizens themselves, not for the benefit of super-rich countries – three years

Many rich people of our country would not have paid either any income tax in their life or paid drastically low amounts compared to what really should be according to their real incomes. This needs to be changed. Proper taxation policies need to be formulated and implemented. The tax money should be utilized for the benefit of all the citizens.

This can be achieved by introducing new tax slabs with a view to uplift the living standard of the middle/lower class and small/ medium businesses. Some of the required measures are below:

- All incomes registered through banks.

- No income tax till 1 lakh rupees income per month.
- Only one tax on income (exceptions for refunds, etc.), no other tax.

See more details later.

Public Contact with MPs/MLAs

G16. Saturdays, Sundays public meetings of elected representatives with public all over India for monitoring, suggestions and directions by citizens and immediate actions by the representatives, so that the citizens become more participants and less spectators – eight months

Once elections are over, how many people would have seen their beloved elected MPs, MLAs or other elected people? The elected representatives become so busy after the elections that they don't have any time for the public.

To change this, Saturdays and Sundays will be reserved for public meetings of the elected representatives with the public all over India. In these meetings, public will give the directions and feedback, and elected representatives will have to take actions according to the feedback received from the public, thus making the public responsible for the type of governance it needs.

Political System

G17. Political system reforms for Loksabha, Vidhansabha, Rajyasabha, Governor, etc., so that the public money is not wasted – two years

Many people would have some idea about what goes on in Loksabha by either having read in the newspapers about or heard on radio about or seen on TV the theatrical dramas, verbal and physical violence, etc., which go on in Loksabha. But most of the people would not know what happens in Rajyasabha except the fact that if the political leaders are pleased with someone and want to favour him/her, he/she gets to Rajysabha and gets salaries, privileges, etc. Similarly, what goes on in Vidhansabha may be similar to Loksabha. It needs to be re-evaluated what is useful and what is pure wastage of public money, and accordingly reforms need to be carried out, so that the best system is offered to the public.

One major flaw in the constitution is to have several political parties which are in total disagreement on most of the issues and have opposing views trying to govern the country in central government and state governments. Having many political parties as different governments in one country is one of the main sources of corruption, where Central government claims to have allocated funds for people in different states but the state governments complain that the funds are not allocated, and so, no benefits occur for the people. Much of the money is absorbed by the corrupt people in the central and state governments.

To change this situation, one major modification is required in the constitution for Loksabha and Vidhansabha: There should be only one election in which each Loksabha candidate will have a list of about 10 candidates attached. The attached candidates will be Vidhansabha candidates. The MPs who win the elections will go to Loksabha. The party that wins majority in Loksabha will send all their Vidhansabha candidates (from the list of attached candidates to Loksabha candidate) to all the Vidhansabhas in the whole country. That means all the Vidhansabhas will have the same party as in the Central government and only one party will be responsible for both Central and all the state governments.

Another change in voting system should be to make the voting requirement not for one party/candidate but for two parties/candidates, the second choice being for the second preference and so requiring to take into account the second preference at 50 per cent value along with the first preference at 100 per cent value and thus counting both the votes of first and second preference to get the overall votes count.

Others:

- Compulsory voting for all the voters.

Hygiene and Cleanliness

G18. Cleanliness, hygiene 100 times better, 2 lakh rose/other flower gardens – two years

Even some of the best places in Delhi and Mumbai, where many tourists also visit, stink of human urine and excretion. The conditions of slum areas where humans live, can be well imagined. One of the very important requirement in the Indian environment is hygiene and cleanliness. Also, lakhs of rose/other flower gardens are needed for public. These gardens should use organic fertilisers which can help human/animal waste management at grand scale.

Natural Disaster Help

G19. Immediate help in case of disaster like flood, earthquake, etc., no deaths due to floods, summer heat or cold in winter – two years

Whenever there is any natural disaster like flood, or earthquake, etc., it is the poor who suffer the most. Thousands of people die every year because of extreme weather – rains, heat or cold. There is a need of setting up of multiple disaster help centers equipped with all the latest equipment, so that immediate help can be provided by the government in the disaster affected areas without any charitable international help. There should not be any deaths due to floods, hot summer or cold winter and no international help should be needed for handling the disasters quickly.

Crime Eradication

G20. Zero crime and 100 times faster justice system– eight years

New and modern techniques, equipment and methods are needed to check the rampant crime which has to be reduced to zero. The justice system in India is so slow and it takes such a long time that it seems that time has no value. With proper increase in justice infrastructure, it is possible to make the justice machinery quicker. Also, the police force needs to be trained and equipped properly to serve the people better. Their number needs to be in proportion to the population, about 3 to 5 per cent of the population. At the same time, they need to be closely monitored for their performance and quick actions are required to be taken against them for any negligence, excess, or unjust actions on their part.

Reservation Policy Solution

G21. 100 times better solutions for reservation policy leading to abolition of reservation – two years

The current reservation policy is full of flaws. It encourages the outdated caste system. Effective and solid steps to improve the living standard of the majority of people who are very poor, need to be taken. Many of them are mentioned in the goals which will help raise the living standard of all and hence will not need any reservation policy. See more details in other items.

Pollution Control

G22. Strict control of noise, industrial, emission and other pollution, and massive reduction in pollution– four years

There is so much of pollution of different types that we need very strict checks to control all the types of pollutions.

Measures to ban the toxic and hazardous industrial waste into rivers are required. At the same time, massive cleaning of rivers is needed. Effective steps need to be taken to clean the rivers and maintain their cleanliness.

Progress through Research

G23. Research Centres for energy, information and communication technology, health and pharmaceutical, aeronautics, transport, bio-technology, defense, intelligent systems, heavy machines, semiconductor, security, etc. – eight years

Research centres for different areas will help to achieve the goals and will make India self-dependent. At the same time, the products manufactured by India based on the Indian research will be sold everywhere in the world bringing wealth in the country and making the people of India prosperous. This will ensure high employment opportunities in India for all the Indians.

Public Entertainment

G24. 10 thousand fun/entertainment parks – four years

For entertainment in the free time for the public and especially children, 10 thousand very high quality fun/entertainment parks with the latest advanced equipment should be made available.

Agriculture Output

G25. Agriculture output 20 times more – four years

Agriculture output needs to be increased by modern agriculture techniques and equipment. Effective methods need to be adapted to increase the agriculture area in the country by identifying suitable land and converting it into agricultural land without disturbing the ecological balance.

Food Quality

G26. Zero food adulteration – one year

We need strict laws, rigorous monitoring and quick punishment actions to stop food adulteration completely.

Children Welfare

G27. Zero child labour – one year

Child labour needs to be stopped completely. Children should be studying in schools, not working.

Poverty Eradication

G28. Zero poverty – four years

All the goals will reduce the poverty which would completely disappear by providing the best education and employment opportunities to all.

India's Self-Confidence

G29. Withdrawal from the ex-slaves club (commonwealth) – eight months

Commonwealth is a club of ex-English colonial countries from where, we should withdraw immediately as we are independent now.

Indian Currency Value

G30. Indian Rupee the topmost currency of the world – eight years

With the achievements of all the goals of the unique transformation programme by the implementation of huge projects, Indian Rupee will become the topmost currency of the world.

Help Centers

G31. Special help centers for farmers, women, emergency, crime; availability of doctors/chemists on weekends/holidays/nights – one year

Special help centers should be set-up all over the country for farmers and women, and for emergency services, crime, etc.

Doctors and chemists should be available on weekends, holidays and at night everywhere in India.

Wildlife and Tourism

G32. Wildlife protection and tourism promotion for foreigners/Indians – eight years

We need to protect the wildlife available in India and this can be made a source of earning of foreign currency by promoting the tourism of foreigners on a large scale. We will have to take the suitable steps in this direction: tourism campaigns in the foreign countries, ensuring the safety of tourists, arrangements of top-class transport and stay facilities in hotels for the tourists. At the same time, Indians should be encouraged to enjoy these tourism facilities which will be enabled by their increased earnings because of better standard of life achieved through other actions of the unique transformation program. Increased tourism by foreign/Indian tourists will increase the employment opportunities naturally.

Healthy Society

G33. Control on drugs, vulgarity and obscenity in public – one year

Evils like drugs which spoil the youth and consequently the nation, and others like vulgarity and obscenity in public, for example, on TV channels or other public places needs to be completely stopped. Strict control and actions are required to be taken in this direction.

11

Implementation Strategy: Huge Projects and Solutions

Huge Projects and Solutions

Why is it so that if an ordinary worker, teacher, or nurse working in India wishes to travel abroad, he/she will have to spend an amount equivalent to about 8 to 10 months' salary to buy the ticket, while for a person of the same category working in West Europe or USA, it is about 15 days' salary? Similarly, the price of a small car is about 10 months' and 5 months' salary respectively. This is linked with the low salaries of people in our country because they do low productivity jobs to fulfil the needs of All Wealth and Talent Drain system described earlier.

This needs to be changed by the following huge projects and solutions which will offer unlimited high productivity jobs with much higher salaries than now to become equal to the developed nations' salary levels.

India has a huge requirement of its own facilities – research and development, design and manufacturing. When we manufacture our own equipment – designed and developed ourselves, we will not have to buy it from outside and at the same time, the foreign countries will be buying the equipment from India. This will automatically raise the value of Indian Rupee increasing it to make it equal to the value of Euro or more. On the contrary, if we don't manufacture our own equipment, we will continue to spend the money, which should be spent on the welfare of Indians, to buy from foreign countries and so, continue to deprive the population of the welfare which it deserves.

All the huge projects and solutions are required in order to achieve all the ultimate extraordinary goals which will lead to achieve the one ultimate top goal of raising the living standard of all the population to move India in the top 10 of the UN Human Development Index. The huge projects and solutions implementation will be directed/monitored by the steering/ monitoring committee of the transformation program.

Advanced High Technology Defense Equipment

S1. L44 fighter plane (2xF22), helicopter, submarine, tank, missile, warship, aircraft carrier, radar, all defense equipment more advanced than the current best technology – eight years

With so much abundance of engineers and scientists, India is capable of designing and manufacturing all the advanced technology equipment for its defense needs. Once the equipment is designed and manufactured in India, first of all, it will be available locally to fulfil the Indian needs leading to huge savings. At the same time, it will be sold to the other countries of the world, providing a source of national income. Both the savings and the incomes can be utilized for the welfare of citizens.

High Speed Airplane

S2. 500 seats, 3000 Km/hour airplane, 600 airports, 30 international airports – eight years

Very simply described, an airplane whether fighter or civil, is a structure designed according to the aerodynamics rules, made of several metallic and/or synthetic material pieces joined together with some mechanical processes, fitted with equipment like motors and air-conditioning/air-pressure control systems, electronic/computer/instrumentation hardware and software, and some furniture. India produces thousands of electrical, electronics, computer, aerodynamics, mechanical and other engineers. What is that talent for? If we can't use the engineers to make the airplanes, we are forced to buy them from foreign companies at exorbitant prices. If we have our own planes, we can not only use them for ourselves to fulfil our huge requirements, but also sell to the whole world, increasing the nation's income. The money thus earned will be used for the prosperity and welfare of citizens.

At the same time, air-travel should be made cheaper and available to majority of the population by constructing about 600 airports. Also, about 30 international airports should be constructed, at least one in each state.

Very High-speed Trains

S3. 600km/hour fast trains five hours journey from Kashmir to Kanyakumari, five hours from Amritsar to Imphal – eight years

The Indian rail system is quite outdated and needs to be changed to a very modern, advanced and comfortable train system. It is possible to have superfast trains all over India reducing the time of travel immensely, e.g., from Srinagar to Kanyakumari in 5 hours and from Amritsar to Imphal in 5 hours.

Space

S4. Manned exploration/space lab for other solar systems, intermediate destination Mars – twelve years

India needs to come forward in the area of space exploration which will provide jobs to thousands of Indians. We should set-up our own space lab for exploration of other solar systems, intermediate destination should be Mars.

Energy

S5. 50 per cent solar, 50 per cent nuclear fusion energy, hydrogen, other, 100 nuclear reactors – eight years

India is blessed with so much sun and is so far behind to use this generous gift of nature, that it is a shame that the solar energy is practically not used according to its available capacity. In fact, more than 50 per cent of the Indian needs of energy can be met by the abundant sunshine available. At the same time, new fusion, hydrogen and other sources of energy need to be explored and deployed to meet the tremendously required energy needs of the country. About 100 nuclear reactors should be installed all over the country to meet the huge power needs.

Telecom

S6. Telecom research, own telecom equipment, all households optical connection – four years

There is a big potential of designing and manufacturing the big and small telecom equipment, thus eliminating the need to buy from foreign countries which is a drain of public money. Even countries like China are manufacturing and selling the switching equipment to India, why not develop and manufacture our own?

Supercomputers

S7. Indian PC, supercomputer – four years

India has the brains to develop its own computers, both small and big supercomputers. This development needs to be planned and organized and it can be done very quickly. What is the engineering talent for, if it is not utilized to design, develop and manufacture our own supercomputers?

Education Facilities

S8. 200 IIT's, 200 AIIMS's, 200 IIM's, 60 thousand medium/low-skill (technical/non-technical) professional schools, 1.8 lakh public libraries and reading-rooms – four years

India has about 50 crores of young people who need the best education facilities at all the levels. For this, there is a huge need of the best education institutes, colleges, universities and schools for different domains. If the facilities are available and the education is provided cheaply to all the young people, there will not be any need of reservation based on castes.

Also, education is the basis for increased employability of all the citizens. In order to make the no entrance test system possible for all the higher education for all the students, about 200 IIT's, AIIM's and IIM's each of the highest standard should be set up all over the country.

At the same time, about 60 thousand medium/low-skill (technical/non-technical) professional schools, 1.8 lakh public libraries and reading-rooms need to be set-up.

Sport Facilities

S9. One lakh sport clubs for all the children, young and old persons, 20 thousand top sports schools, 60 thousand swimming pools, one lakh fitness centers two years

To obtain a gold medal in Olympics, it needs about 10 years of hard-work and training. The children have to be provided top-class sport facilities, so that they can show their talents to win the gold medals. At the same time, sport facilities will help to improve the general health of the citizens, both young and old, thus reducing the chances of becoming ill and so, increasing the average life expectancy. To obtain about 200 Olympic gold medals, about one lakh sport clubs, 60 thousand swimming pools, one lakh fitness centers, 20 thousand top sports schools should be set-up. Regular tournaments in the various sports disciplines should be organized all over India. This will also increase the employment opportunities.

Health Care

S10. 60 thousand top class hospitals – four years

With its large population, India needs a big number of top class hospitals, so that the citizens' health is taken care of with utmost care. At present, only one or two top-class hospitals are available in only very big cities. These hospitals are overcrowded because the population of the big cities has increased enormously. The situation in medium and small cities can well be imagined. We need to provide the best health care to 100 per cent of the population, that means, a huge number of high-quality hospitals, about 60 thousand, with all the best, modern equipment and providing almost free medical facilities to all the citizens are needed.

Innovative Products

S11. Innovative product development, cyclone prevention, weather control, future travel, etc. – eight years

In India, we miss the innovative ideas. A very simple example is of bicycle. Bicycle is one of the most used means of transport all over India for many years. But over the many years, there has been only one model available with practically no accessories, for example, for carrying the children. In western world, they have made several models of bicycles to meet different types of needs like bicycles with gears, for mountains, etc. At the same type, different types of carriages for children are in the market there. The western mind looks always for improvements and innovation which is lacking in India. We must encourage the growth of innovative ideas and their conversion into new products, the improvement of the existing products should take place at the same time.

Luxury Car and Modern Bus

S12. Indian luxury car, comfortable bus – eight years

India should develop and manufacture its own cars for its own market instead of buying from abroad. Car is a very small machine which can be very easily designed by the mechanical, electrical, electronic and computer engineers who are available in plenty in India. Why not use these engineers?

Telescope

S13. World's biggest land/space telescope – eight years

For astronomical and space research, India should build the world's biggest land/space telescope.

Electronic Chips

S14. Micro/nano-chips development – four years

For all the advanced equipment, India should have its own chip development and manufacturing facilities.

Medical Equipment

S15. All latest medical instruments, more advanced than the current best technology – four years

There is huge need of all Indian advanced and high-quality medical equipment for Indian market. These equipment, once developed and manufactured in India, can be sold to foreign countries, resulting in huge incomes for India.

Heavy Machines

S16. All heavy industrial machines, road building machines, cranes, CNC, others – eight years

All the advanced heavy industrial machines should be developed and manufactured in India as there is a huge requirement of all these machines in India.

Appliances

S17. Consumer electronics, home appliances – eight years

India needs its own electronic and home appliances for its own needs.

Environment

S18. Filth and environment management – two years

Many places in India in all the cities and villages are full of squalor and garbage, lacking basic sanitation and hygiene. Many people are forced to live in these deplorable conditions. This gives rise to many diseases. To change this, a very powerful filth and environment management is needed all over India, to make India the cleanest country in the world.

Also, special steps are needed for protection and conservation of Tribal regions, forests and wild life of the country.

Disaster Help Centers

S19. 60 thousand well-equipped disaster help/recovery centers – two years

Every year, natural disasters like flood, earthquake, etc., occur in some or the other parts of India. We need huge number of very well equipped natural disaster help and recovery centers all over India, to save human life and properties in case of natural calamities.

Judicial System

S20. 50 times increase in judicial system infrastructure, courts, judges, staff, etc. – three years

India with its huge population and high crime rate needs an improved and fast judicial system which can be possible by improving and modernizing the judicial infrastructure. The crime has to be checked by quick and severe punishments.

Social Care System

S21. New social department linked with tax, employment, education, internal security, housing departments - one year

To manage properly, we need a sophisticated social care system. This will provide the basis of better life for all – education, sports, health, employment, no crime, better life, etc. India (about 30 lakh sq. km) needs to be divided in 60 thousand Managed Zones units which would be of maximum about 50 sq. km. size and/or maximum about 20 thousand population each. For each of these units, the following 13 persons will be responsible to take care of the population in the area of the unit:

- one social worker who will take care of the needs of education, sports, employment, health, housing, security, pension, etc.
- one administration worker to take care of all the administration – birth/death registration/certificates, passport
- one infrastructure worker to take care of all the infrastructure like roads, transport, education, sports, hospitals, judicial help, electricity, water, gas, etc.
- one tax worker to control the tax payments
- one police worker to provide the security
- one medical doctor to take care of the health
- one responsible for pollution control
- one responsible for garbage management
- one responsible for traffic management
- one responsible for culture
- one responsible for sports
- one MLA to coordinate and monitor
- one senior general management consultant to co-ordinate all the activities and report to the national program execution and monitoring authority

The above 13 persons will be the backbone of all the changes to be introduced. They will be connected by a mobile video Virtual Private Network to the monitoring committee by mobile video telephony and will be continuously contacted and monitored. Any complaint of any citizen in any unit will be attended very quickly by this system and the standard of life of all the citizens will be improved by this social care system. People's needs will be analyzed and the solutions provided with the help of a huge country database to keep track of each citizen and permanent monitoring.

All the 60 thousand Managed Zones will work for the assigned tasks as the different cells work in the human body. A monitoring network consisting of about 70 thousand general management consultants will work as the sensory network of the human body. This will provide inputs and feedback to the monitoring center which will act as the controlling brain of the body. Monitoring center will interact with the executive control part, that is the government, which will take actions for corrections in the Managed Zones.

Music and Art

S22. 60 thousand music schools, Indian classic (India instruments, south, north, Rabindra sangeet)/western classic (piano, violin, cello, oboe, mandolin, orchestra), 60 thousand arts schools, 1.2 lakh auditoriums – two years

Music and art are an important aspect of life and this aspect needs to be taken care of by a huge number of schools equipped with all the facilities. Attending these schools will encourage the children, young and old people to appreciate the life better. At the same time, regular cultural programs will be organized by the students of these schools. All this will also increase the employment opportunities linked with the musical/cultural activities. In this regard, 60 thousand music schools, 60 thousand arts schools and 1.2 lakh auditoriums should be set-up.

Public Toilets

S23. 20 lakh extremely clean and hygienic public toilets, out of which 1 lakh each in 10 big cities, 3 persons per sq. km to maintain cleanliness – two years

Many places all over the cities and villages are open toilets for a huge number of citizens. This primitive way of open toilets for humans needs to be changed to the modern way of hygienic toilets with proper sewer and drainage connection. Many diseases can be prevented automatically by proper toilet facilities all over the country. Huge number of hygienic toilets (about 20 lakhs) needs to be built all over India. Also, three persons per sq. km are required to maintain general cleanliness all over India all the time, that means about 1 crore persons for this job are required.

Agriculture Research

S24. Agricultural research and reforms, better, advanced farming techniques, subsidies, financial help for farmers – three years

Majority of Indian farmers are busy toiling in their fields with their century old techniques. With major research in the area of agriculture, a lot of improvement in agriculture output is needed. At the same time, policies need to be introduced for the benefit and safeguarding the interests of hard-working farmers and consumers, to eradicate the middlemen in agricultural market, to transport farm products to and sell them in the markets.

Full immediate attention shall be paid to farmer suicides and conditions will be created to eliminate this scourge from our society.

Milk Dairies

S25. 60 thousand cheap, big, high-quality supermarkets to keep prices under control and 10 thousand modern milk dairies – three years

All over India, 60 thousand cheap and big supermarkets with the highest quality products are required for the public. Similarly, milk and milk products are the much needed nutrients to increase the height of people, and for this, a huge number of modern dairies, about 10 thousand, are needed. The supermarkets and milk dairies will be set up all over the country.

Zero Black Money and Zero Tax Evasion by On-line Payment Network

S26. On-line payment network with 30 lakh on-line payment service centers and three lakh bank branches – two years

Zero black money and zero tax-evasion can be achieved by the implementation of Zero Black money and zero Tax-evasion System (ZBTS) which consists of an extensive on-line payment network with 30 lakh on-line payment service centers and 3 lakh bank branches. This can be achieved within about two years. See the description of this system in the chapter 17B Zero Black Money and Zero Tax-evasion System.

Nutrition

S27. 60 thousand high quality, cheap, clean and hygienic public restaurants – one year

This will make good and high quality prepared food available for general public. At the same time, it will provide employment opportunities to lakhs of people all over India.

Engineering Education Review and Evolution

S28. New technology-oriented suitable cross-discipline engineering education – one year

Our engineering education needs to be reviewed and evolved suitably to take care of the evolving technology, for example, new techniques in the construction engineering, cross-discipline studies such as combination of nano-technology/chip-technology and mechanical/medical engineering, bio-technology, etc. to fulfil the needs of new systems' and equipment's design in mechanical/ medical areas, etc., require a serious review and evolution of the engineering education.

Hotels for Tourism

S29. 30 thousand top quality hotels, 30 to 50 times more foreign tourists – two years

Number of foreign tourists can be increased significantly by appropriate steps which are developing the best tourism infrastructure for stay and transport of the tourists, both foreigners and Indians. About 30 thousand top quality hotels are needed for this purpose. Tourism campaigns both in India for Indians and in foreign countries for the foreigners are needed to be organized to expose the vast tourism potential in India. Increase in foreign tourists will earn foreign currency which can be used to buy essential items that are not available in India like petrol from abroad instead of using cheap IT and non IT-labour to earn foreign currency.

Professionals Migration

S30. Professional migration compensation from the immigration country – two years

As many developed countries receive fully formed – educated, trained, experienced – professional immigrants – engineers, doctors, lawyers, pilots, managers, hotel specialists, etc. – from India for whose formation India has spent a lot of money and the immigrant countries have spent nothing, the immigrant countries should be asked to pay one million Euros for each professional migrant migrating to the immigrant country permanently. For temporary migration of the professionals, this amount should be 0.5 million Euros.

12

People

People Characteristics

All the elected representatives (Municipality, MLA or MP) who will be responsible for the implementation of the unique transformation program should have the following characteristics:

1. Sympathetic to the 70 per cent of the low income fellow citizens.
2. Committed to real service to the people and working in a selfless manner to raise the living conditions of all the population, especially 70 per cent low income holders.
3. No criminal record.
4. Assets should be proportional to the income.
5. Committed not to indulge in corruption or black money.
6. In sound health.
7. Mentally strong.
8. Age group between 25 to 75 years.
9. Education at least graduation with sound knowledge of either Hindi or English: better if both.
10. Should have strong feeling of nationalism
11. Committed for zero corruption everywhere.
12. A clean record with no previous litigations/prosecutions in court of law.
13. Gentle and respected in society.

14. Disciplined character without any kind of ego.
15. Have working knowledge of computer and internet.
16. Good communication skills.
17. Have secular feelings.
18. Tolerant for all religions without any kind of hatred to any caste, sect or religion.
19. Should have no superiority or inferiority feelings/complex.
20. Should be fully committed to support the implementation of the unique transformation program for the welfare and upliftment of the living standard of all the 100 per cent population.

13

Basic Policies

Basic Policies

Following should be the Basic Policies of the political leaders to implement the unique transformation program:

1. Should be strongly and fully committed to the implementation of the unique transformation program providing complete solutions to all the citizens' and nation's problems by providing all the best facilities to all the 100 per cent population at all the places in all the domains with special attention for the lower 70 per cent income group, weaker sections, women, farmers and rural areas.
2. Should be strongly and fully committed and competent to eradicate fully all corruption, crime, black money, poverty, hunger, unemployment, illiteracy, tax evasion, malnutrition, exploitation, heavy price rise, food adulteration, farmer suicide, crime against women and girls, child labour, drugs and other evils of the society.
3. For corruption-free working, all the party workers, elected representatives, government employees/officers shall have their Terms of Collaboration: details of their work and compensation (salary/bonus/facilities). None of them shall have any right over anything more than that from anywhere because of the position. Huge amount of money may pass through these individuals for public projects, but nobody

shall have any right to take even a single paisa from that money for private use.

4. Strict supervision, monitoring and quick actions for honest, corruption-free, citizen-friendly, smooth governance shall be provided.
5. All the excellent features in the unique transformation program regarding health, black-money, tax-evasion, crime, etc., which are not available in even the developed West European countries shall be provided.

14

Basic Strategic Outline

Basic Strategic Outline

Sustainable ZERO corruption processes for making India free of corruption/hunger/poverty/crime/black money/tax evasion

Following is the summary of basic strategic framework according to what has been described earlier:

Four salient features:

1. Simple rules
2. Political/administration reforms
3. Strict monitoring and control
4. Quick corrective actions

Rules:

1. All the elected representatives, government employees/ officers, political party workers shall adhere to the basic policies (see chapter 13 Basic Policies).
2. All the major projects mentioned in the chapter 15, List of Major Projects and all the major systems, sub-systems and programs mentioned in the chapter 17 Main Systems, Sub-systems and Programmes should be implemented.

Political/Administration Reforms:

1. 30 lakh sq. km should be divided into 60 thousand Managed Zones of about 50 sq. km each (about 20 thousand population)
2. 13 responsible for:
    a. administration: to take care of all administration – birth/ death registration/certificates, passport, driving license, etc.
    b. social needs: to take care of the needs of education, sports, employment, health, housing, security, pension, etc.
    c. infrastructure: to take care of all the infrastructure like roads, transport, education, sports, hospitals, judicial help, electricity, water, gas, etc.
    d. tax: to control the tax payments
    e. police: to provide security to about 4 to 5 per cent of the population as the number of police staff
    f. medical: to take care of the health
    g. pollution control
    h. garbage management
    i. traffic management
    j. cultural activities
    k. sports management
    l. one MLA to coordinate and monitor
    m. one senior general management consultant to co-ordinate all the activities and report to the national program execution and monitoring authority
3. Elections:
    a. One election
    b. MLAs linked to MPs
    c. Majority party to run all the states with the linked list of MLAs
    d. Lokpal direct election

4. Rajyasabha members – the function and utility of Rajyasabha, Vidhansabha and Vidhanparishad to be analyzed and reviewed, and their functions to be changed:
   a. only 100
   b. direct election
   c. work as Lokayukt

Monitoring/control and actions by monitoring/controlling committee:

1. Connection of 60,000x13 responsible plus the monitoring/controlling personnel by mobile video VPN.
2. All citizens database, their needs (education, health, transport, sports, etc.)
3. National complaint centers for public complaints
4. Control room for
   a. constant monitoring of quality of life and needs of population
   b. continuous monitoring of crimes, illegal money transactions
   c. quick actions on issues of quality of life, crimes, illegal money transactions

15

List of Major Projects

List of Major Projects

Following is the list of major projects to implement the unique transformation programme based on and according to the descriptions in the earlier chapters:

1. Reforms

a. Education

i. Children till six years: only sports, arts, music, foreign/regional languages, yoga classes
ii. No entrance exam anywhere for any higher education with tremendous increase in the education facilities
iii. Change in exam system: exam based on understanding, analysis and application skills, not on only memory power
iv. Engineering education evolution with inter-disciplinary engineering education

b. Tax

i. Simple tax rules proportional to incomes and their implementation, no tax for low incomes.

2. Managed Zones

a. Managed Zones definition, buildings, 13 responsible assignment

b. Integrated IT applications for all the 13 departments

3. Zero corruption

a. Mobile Video VPN connection of all the 13 responsibles of all the Managed with the monitoring/controlling center

4. Citizen Care

a. Citizen database to take care of all the citizens needs

5. Education

a. Primary schools
b. Secondary schools
c. Colleges
d. Universities
e. Medium/low-skill (technical/non-technical) professional schools
f. IITs
g. IIMs
h. AIIMSs
i. Libraries, reading rooms

6. Transport

a. Road network
b. Modern bus
c. Small taxi in place of 3-wheelers
d. Rail network
e. International airports
f. Domestic airports
g. Frequent transport services within the city (by road/rail), and intercity (by road/rail/air)
h. Trained, polite and, friendly staff
i. Pollution free vehicles
j. No car and motor zones near the center town areas and shopping areas, connectivity by cycle rickshaws, cycles to nearest parking stands for the motors.

7. Traffic

a. Parking stands for motor vehicles to be located near metro stations, railway stations, center town areas, shopping areas
b. Pedestrian crossings
c. Traffic signs
d. Strict traffic rules
e. Speed/drink control checks

8. Health

a. Hospitals
b. Patient care – ambulance services, 24x7 chemist/doctor availability, medical information pamphlets, cheap medicines, others

9. Housing

a. Housing for all the population
b. 24-hours electricity, water, gas connection
c. Migrant workers housing
d. Massive tree plantation in and around housing areas

10. Sports

a. Sport halls
b. Sport clubs
c. Top sport schools
d. Athletic tracks
e. Sport fields
f. Fitness centers
g. Olympic gold medal training

11. Safety

a. Disaster help/recovery centers

12. Justice

a. Judicial system improvements

13. Culture

a. Music schools (Indian/Western classic)
b. Auditoriums
c. Top musician formation

14. Hygiene

a. Public toilets
b. Clean public places/roads

15. Price control

a. Supermarkets
b. Milk dairies

16. Governance transparency

a. Transparency through internet information

17. Environment

a. Pollution control (all industrial/vehicle emission/noise/ river pollution)
b. Rose/flowers gardens
c. Tree plantation

18. Shopping

a. Shopping centers

19. Security

a. Trained, polite, friendly police
b. Women safety
c. Defense/judicial staff increase

20. Entertainment

a. Fun/entertainment parks
b. Sports/culture TV channel

21. Comfort

a. Proper scheduling of flights, no flights during night to reduce noise for the people living near the airports

22. Waste management

a. Garbage collection/disposal management
b. Sewer system

23. Help desk

a. Help desks for all the problems, complaints

24. Work conditions

a. Working hours
b. Crèches for children

25. Old age help

a. Old age homes

26. Energy

a. Solar energy
b. Nuclear reactors

27. Research centers

a. Weather
b. Nano-technology
c. Agriculture
d. Medicine – malaria, cancer, aids
e. Very high speed train
f. Supercomputer
g. Telecom
h. Home appliances
i. Automation
j. Innovative products
k. Defense equipment
l. Medical equipment

m. Heavy machines
n. Nuclear fusion technology

28. Public meetings

a. Public meetings feedback and actions

29. New manufacturing industries

a. Airplane
b. High speed train
c. Supercomputer
d. Custom chip design and manufacturing

30. Zero black money, zero tax evasion

a. On-line payment network
b. Banks and bank accounts
c. Tax deduction from the income in the banks

31. Nutrition

a. Food adulteration prevention and control
b. Restaurants
c. Quality control (cleanliness and hygiene) in all types of food stalls

32. Water resources

a. Water canal/reservoir/pumping/purification network

33. Professional migration

a. Professional migration compensation from the immigration country

16

Strategy Implementation Model and Formulae

Strategy Implementation Model and Formulae

The following formulae are based on already available, well-implemented, proven models in the developed West European countries. These can be used for miraculously fast and balanced development in India to raise the living standard by about 100 times of 100 per cent of the population living everywhere in India.

Facilities/infrastructure calculation for Managed Zones:

India should be divided in about 60 thousand managed zones, each managed zone consisting of area about 50 sq. km, population about 20 thousand, population density about 400.

According to the Transformation Programme contents:

1. Managed Zone management:

For each managed zone, the following strictly monitored offices with trained staff will be established:

a. Administration – birth/death registration/certificates, passport, driving license, etc.

b. Social needs – education, sports, employment, health, housing, security, pension, etc.
c. Infrastructure control – roads, transport, education, sports, hospitals, judicial help, electricity, water, gas, etc.
d. Tax
e. Police
f. Health
g. Pollution
h. Garbage
i. Traffic
j. Culture
k. Sports
l. MLA
m. General management consultant for monitoring /co-ordination.

In the list which follows, the numbers indicate the applicable quantity for one managed zone. Numbers less than 1 indicate that more than one managed zones are concerned.

2. Zero corruption:

a. All the above responsible persons connected by mobile video VPN (Virtual Private Network) for strict monitoring and control. General management consultant network working for monitoring/co-ordination/feedback

3. Citizen care:

a. All the citizens registered in a database for monitoring their social, educational, health and other needs for taking the right actions for their welfare

4. Education:

a. 10 primary, 10 secondary very high-quality schools
b. 10 very high standard colleges
c. 0.03 universities
d. Extra-help in study for weak students
e. New: 0.01 IITs, 0.01 AIIMSs, 0.01 IIMs

f. 7 medium/low-skill (technical/non-technical) professional schools
g. Crèches/schools for temporary migrant workers children
h. Foreign/regional language classes for children
i. Yoga classes for children
j. 3 books/cd libraries/reading rooms
k. Inter-disciplinary engineering education: chip design + mechanical/medical/.

5. Transport:

a. Much better road layout standards (West-European style) with trees, flowers, separate pedestrian, bicycle paths
b. Road construction according to new road layout standards on at least 20 per cent area of each managed zone
c. Extensive road network of highways, national roads and local roads
d. Much better buses of international standard
e. Much better, trained, polite, helpful bus staff
f. 5 to 10 times increase in frequency of buses according to the requirement of individual route
g. Cheaper, better taxi service
h. Replacement of 3-wheelers by small taxis
i. Replacement of manual rickshaws by motor-driven rickshaws
j. Point-to-point bus transport system for office goers reducing the private car traffic
k. Fast train connections for medium cities to nearby cities of other managed zones
l. Battery operated vehicles for inner city
m. .01 airport
n. New international airports

6. Traffic:

a. 4 underground/multistoreyed parking of 100 to 1000 places
b. Strict traffic/driving rules

c. 10 sq. km roads (20 per cent of 50 sq. km) connecting each house/apartment to the state road network
d. 200 pedestrian crossings
e. Extensive traffic signs
f. Road markings on all the roads
g. Special traffic police with strict monitoring/training
h. Frequent & strict speed control checks
i. Frequent & strict drink control checks

7. Health:

a. 1 top class hospital
b. Free doctor house visit for 50+ health check-up/follow-up (not even in Europe)
c. Cheap medicines
d. Chemist shop/doctor available on Sunday/holiday/night
e. Effective and quick ambulance service
f. Home help for handicapped/seriously ill/old people
g. Disease prevention information pamphlets for free distribution

8. Housing:

a. Decent housing with toilet for all the families, no slums
b. 24-hours electricity, water, gas connection
c. All houses connected by road to state road network
d. Social housing for economic weaker section
e. Temporary migrant worker's housing

9. Sports:

a. 10 sport clubs
b. 2 sport halls for indoor games – badminton, volley ball, basketball, gymnasium
c. 1 top sport school
d. 1 athletic tracks
e. 2 football/hockey fields
f. 2 tennis fields with 5 to 10 courts
g. 0.002 Olympic gold medals target

h. 0.02 world top badminton, tennis, table tennis players each (1200 in 60K units)
i. 0.002 world top hockey, football, volleyball, basketball, gymnasium, athletic teams each (120 in 60K units)
j. 1 fitness center

10. Safety:

a. 2 well-equipped disaster help/recovery centers
b. Emergency help at railway stations, airport, all public places
c. All electric cables underground, no open naked cables anywhere
d. No open drainage holes anywhere

11. Justice:

a. 10 to 20 times increase in judicial system infrastructure, courts, judges, staff etc., for quick justice

12. Culture:

a. 4 music schools, Indian classic (Indian instruments, south, north, rabindra sangit)/western classic (piano, violin, cello, oboe, mandolin, orchestra)
b. 2 auditoriums of 100 to 800 seats
c. 1 top Sitar player and flute player each
d. 0.3 Indian classic music orchestras
e. 1 world top western classic pianists, violin, cello players each
f. 0.3 western classic music orchestras

13. Hygiene:

a. 100 extremely clean and hygienic public toilets
b. Extremely clean roads and all public places, no garbage anywhere in open places
c. Use of decomposing agents for wastes, bio toilets.

14. Price control:

a. 2 cheap, big, high-quality supermarkets
b. 1 milk dairy

15. Governance transparency:

a. Zero corruption and full transparency in all financial dealings/contracts

16. Environment:

a. Industrial waste disposal control
b. Vehicle emission control
c. Noise pollution control
d. 6 rose/other flowers gardens
e. Massive tree plantation
f. Zero river pollution

17. Shopping:

a. 2 big shopping centers
b. Fixed prices, compulsory price display

18. Security:

a. Increase in police for security with strict monitoring/ training of police to help public, police staff 3 to 5 per cent of the population
b. Special attention for safety of women – heavy day/night patrol of women police
c. Defense staff, 3 to 5 per cent of the population
d. Judicial staff, 5 per cent of the population

19. Entertainment:

a. Sports/culture TV channel
b. 0.2 fun/entertainment parks

20. Comfort:

a. No air-flights take-off and landing at night

21. Waste management:

a. Effective garbage collection/disposal
b. Better sewer system
c. Use of waste decomposing agents.

22. Help desk:

a. Central help desk for all the problems of transport, gas, electricity, garbage collection

23. Better work conditions:

a. 40 hours per week
b. 10 top quality crèches for children of working mothers

24. Old age help:

a. Top quality old age homes for helpless old people

25. Energy:

a. 50-70 per cent solar energy
b. Nuclear reactors

26. Research centers:

a. Weather control
b. Nano-technology
c. Agriculture
d. Medicine – malaria, cancer, AIDS
e. Very high speed train
f. Supercomputer
g. Telecom
h. Home appliances
i. Automation
j. Innovative products – alternative paper
k. Defense equipment
l. Medical equipment
m. Heavy machines
n. Nuclear fusion technology

27. Elected representatives public meetings:

a. Every Saturday/Sunday for public clarifications, discussions, grievances, improvements, suggestions, etc.

28. New industries:

a. Airplane manufacturing
b. High speed train manufacturing

c. Supercomputer manufacturing
d. Custom chip design and manufacturing

29. Zero black money, zero tax evasion:

a. 5 banks
b. Free bank account and bank card for everybody
c. Online payment system for all the businesses, shops, vendors – small, medium and big
d. 50 Online Payment Service Centers (OPSC)
e. All payment by bank card
f. Bank withdrawal limited to Rs 1000 max per month for each family

30. Nutrition:

a. Zero food adulteration
b. 2 very high-quality cheap restaurants

31. Water resources:

a. Extensive canal/reservoir/pumping/purification network

32. Professional migration:

a. Professional migration compensation from the immigration country: 1 million Euros for each Indian permanent migrant and 0.5 million Euros for each Indian temporary migrant

17

Main Systems, Sub-systems and Programmes

Main Systems, Sub-systems and Programmes

Following main systems, sub-systems and programmes are part of the unique transformation programme and are required to be implemented to achieve the ultimate top goal.

A. Execution, Monitoring and Control System (EMCS)

a. Execution Sub-system (ES)
b. Monitoring and Control Sub-system (MCS)
c. Citizen Database (CDB)
d. Mobile Video VPN Sub-system (MVVS)

B. Zero Black money and Zero Tax-evasion System (ZBTS)
C. Automatic Zero Flood/Drought System (AZFDS)
D. Citizen Democratic Participation System (CDPS)
E. Home R&D, Design and Manufacturing Programme (HRDMP)
F. Village Transformation Programme (VTP)

The above systems, sub-systems and programmes are described in the subsequent sub-chapters.

17A

Execution, Monitoring and Control System (EMCS)

Execution, Monitoring and Control System (EMCS)

This is the core system of the unique transformation programme because all the work is carried out by this system. At the same time, monitoring and control is included in the system for its proper functioning. This comprises of the sub-systems mentioned below.

Execution Sub-system (ES)

Similar to human body where all the cells, which combined together form different components of the body, do their assigned work continuously with proper monitoring, feedback and control mechanisms, the whole country will be divided in about 60 thousand managed zones of about 50 square kilometer in size and about 20 thousand population each. Different domains in the managed zone will be looked after by one responsible person each with necessary required supporting staff for that domain in each managed zone, thus total of 13 persons for each managed zone (see chapter 14 Basic Strategic Outline). Out of these, 12 will be directly controlled by the government for execution of all the policies regarding the unique transformation programme. Each responsible person will do his/her assigned work in that domain while interacting with other responsible persons, and will be answerable in the assigned domain for the managed zone.

Monitoring and Control Sub-system (MCS)

Similar to human body where monitoring and control is done by the brain by using the feedback and control by the nerves, strict monitoring, control and co-ordination will be done by a general management consultant network which will consist of the 13th responsible person of the managed zone. This will work as an independent network, the top control of which will be directly linked with the top layer of government execution sub-system mentioned above. Hence, the execution and monitoring/ control sub-systems will work in strong unison and harmony to achieve the desired ultimate top goal.

Citizen Database (CDB)

A complete citizen database with all the information required to fulfil all the functions of the different domains will serve as tool for the authorized persons of the domains in the managed zones.

Mobile Video VPN System (MVVS)

All the 13 responsible persons of different domains in each managed zone will be connected to the top control of the monitoring and control network through Mobile Video VPN System for constant contact, feedback, reporting and actions.

17B

Zero Black Money & Zero Tax-Evasion System (ZBTS)

Zero Black Money & Zero Tax-Evasion System (ZBTS) by On-line Payment Network

Zero black money and zero tax-evasion can be achieved by the implementation of Zero Black money and zero Tax-evasion System (ZBTS) which will consist of an extensive, highly reliable on-line payment network with 30 lakh on-line payment service centers and 3 lakh bank branches. This can be achieved within about 2 years. Following are the features of the ZBTS:

1. All the money transactions shall be done by either bank transfer, or bank draft, or bank/cash card.
2. All the vendors, sellers, shopkeepers, businessmen shall have On-line Payment Terminals (OPT) connected through highly secure and reliable Wi-Fi On-line Payment Network (OPN).
3. 30 lakhs On-line Payment Service Centers (OPSC) to help on-line payment.
4. Minimum 3 lakh bank branches all over India.
5. All citizens shall be required to have a bank account and bank/cash cards for payment.
6. All the businesses small/medium/big shall be required to have a bank account.
7. No bank account holder shall be allowed to withdraw cash more than rupees 1000 per month.
8. All the current cash payments to be done either by bank card or cash card, very small cash payment allowed only in case of emergency.

9. All the money transactions of more than Rs 5 thousand per month for all the accounts shall be reported by all the banks to the Tax responsible (see chapter 14 Basic Strategic Outline).
10. 5 per cent tax on all the bank deposits for all the accounts after a certain threshold, increasing the tax to higher percentage for higher deposits, no other taxes of any kind.
11. All the tax rules to be revised and simplified in favour of low income holders and to have minimum number of taxes.
12. Income threshold for tax to be raised significantly. High tax on high incomes (bank deposits) and extra-high tax on exorbitant incomes (bank deposits).

Advantages of ZBTS:

1. Zero black money.
2. Zero tax evasion.

17C

Automatic Zero Flood/Drought System (AZFDS)

Automatic Zero Flood/Drought System (AZFDS) for automatic water resources control

Advanced, automatic zero flood/drought, zero drinking water shortage and zero river water pollution system with extensive canal/reservoir/pumping/purification network for full water utilization.

Whenever it rains, there are floods in different parts of the country, killing mostly the poor people who don't have any solid shelter. Then, there are droughts when there is no rain and the poor suffer again. With so many rivers and so much of rains, there needs to be designed an automatic massive flood/drought control system to utilize the natural gifts in a suitable and useful manner for the welfare of all the citizens. This can be achieved with planned connection of all the major rivers from north to south and east to west and by designing an advanced, automatic zero flood, zero drinking water shortage and zero river water pollution system with massive canal/reservoir/pumping/purification network as described below.

A. Full water utilization and control advanced features

This modern, automated system with automatic controls, measurements and monitoring will be a unique, powerful, massive water control and utilization system. It will have the following advanced features:

i. Coverage

It will cover the following:

1. Built for about 200 to 300 rivers in India
2. Beneficial for complete 30 lakh square km area of India

ii. Infrastructure construction

The system will use the following network infrastructure which will have to be built:

a. Canal/reservoir/pumping/purification network

The following network of canals, reservoirs, pumps, water purification plants will be built:

1. Water storage tanks
2. River interconnection canal network
3. Water storage gates
4. Canal interconnection gates
5. Canal outlet gates for agriculture use
6. Drinking water purification plants
7. Stoppage of drain/impure/polluted water dumping in rivers
8. Drinking water distribution network to all the houses and buildings

b. Measuring and monitoring network

The following measuring and monitoring network will be built:

1. Rainfall level measurement
2. Storage tank level measurement
3. River water level measurement
4. Canal water level measurement
5. River water purity measurement

iii. Control and monitoring features

The system will have the following automatic controls, measurements and monitoring mechanisms:

a. Automatic controls

The following automatic controls will be used:

1. River water level
2. Rain water storage

3. Water storage gates opening/closing
4. Canal system water distribution
5. Canals interconnection gates opening/closing

b. Automatic measurements and monitoring

The following measurements and monitoring will be done:

1. Rainfall level
2. River water level
3. Storage tank water level
4. Canal water level
5. River water purity level

iv. Quantitative infrastructure analysis

The following quantitative analysis is an approximate assessment of the required infrastructure in terms of the quantity:

a. Canal/reservoir/pumping/purification network infrastructure construction

Following is an approximate infrastructure requirement of the canals, reservoirs, pumps, water purification plants, etc.

1. Underground Storage tanks: about 20 thousand
2. Storage tank gates: about 50 thousand
3. Drinking water purification plants: about 20 thousand
4. Waste/drainage water purification plants: about 20 thousand
5. Canal distribution network 2 to 3 lakh square kms.
6. Canal interconnection gates: about 1 to 2 lakh
7. Drinking water distribution network to all the houses: to cover about 30 crore houses/apartments/buildings

b. Measurements and monitoring network

The following is an approximate requirement of automatic measurement and monitoring network:

1. Rainfall level measurement points: about 10 thousand
2. River water level measurement points: about 20 thousand
3. Storage tank level measurement points: about 20 thousand
4. Canal water level measurement points: about 50 thousand
5. River water purity monitoring points: about 10 thousand

B. Advantages

This system will ensure the following huge advantages for all over India:

1. Zero flood/drought
2. Zero drinking water shortage – 24 hours water availability to all the households and other buildings
3. Sufficient water availability for agriculture everywhere
4. Zero river water pollution
5. Safety of life and property of all the citizens, especially the poor people due to no floods
6. No price rise due to loss of harvest because of no floods and no drought
7. River water purity with no water pollution

17D

Citizen Democratic Participation System (CDPS)

Citizen Democratic Participation System (CDPS)

In order to achieve real democracy where people are true participants in the democratic control of the governing processes, a Citizen Democratic Participation System (CDPS) with the sub-systems mentioned below will be established.

Weekly Public Meeting Feedback and Action Sub-system (WPMFAS)

In order to achieve real democracy where people are true participants in the democratic control of the governing processes, weekly public meetings of all the elected representatives with the people will be organized in each managed zone throughout the year. All the meeting minutes with all the action points, their progress and execution will be entered in the Weekly Public Meeting Feedback and Action System and will be available on internet for consultation. So, all the citizens should be able to see the progress of their requests, complaints, etc., on internet.

Citizens Requirements Request Sub-system (CRRS)

In this sub-system, all the citizens can post their valid requirements and issues which may be concerning their managed zone, village, city, state or at national level. These requirements requests will be constantly monitored by the General management consultant of the managed zone for coordinating the required actions. The actions taken for the requirements and issues will be entered by the relevant authorities and will be possible to be seen by the public.

Citizen Complaint Sub-system (CCS)

It will be possible for all the citizens to lodge a valid complaint against any official of any domain in this sub-system. These complaints will be constantly monitored by the general management consultant of the managed zone for coordinating the required actions. The actions taken for the complaints will be entered by the relevant authorities and will be possible to be seen by the public.

17E

Home R&D, Design and Manufacturing Programme (HRDMP)

Home R&D, Design and Manufacturing Programme (HRDMP)

Underestimation and underutilization of capacity and capability of IITs and Indian talent

One of the areas where India has highly underestimated and huge unutilized capacity is human talent. This resource is so deplorably wasted that there is no comparative example in the world for such a colossal richness and at the same time huge non-utilization and wastage in this domain. The wastage is done firstly, by not providing sufficient opportunities for it to allow to develop and bloom. Secondly, inspite of this, whatever gets developed a significant part is gifted away freely to the already developed world in the form of qualified and experienced professionals' migration to the developed countries, consequently these receiving countries benefit without paying a single rupee to the Indian government for the free gift and without spending a single dollar for the formation and building of the talent capacity in their own countries. Thirdly, by not creating opportunities in India for utilizing the remaining immense talent in the country.

IITs are a huge reservoir of underutilized talent and capacity, and also one of the biggest source of losing highly capable and freely given resource to the outside world in the form of nation's talent drain to the developed countries.

We should encourage brilliant, splendid, dazzling , high-value, innovative ideas which can change the destiny of about 120 crore people and with which the available talent capacity and capability can be utilized to make India a balanced developed country.

Home R&D, Design and Manufacturing Program (HRDMP) for own use and international sale

In order to use the talent of IIT's fully or at least partially, the following Home R&D, Design and Manufacturing Program should be implemented:

Step 1: Highly advanced research centers with close collaboration of the industries, IIT's, top universities, top engineering colleges and medical institutes in the following areas should be setup: energy, information and communication technology, health/medicine, pharmaceutical, aeronautics, transport (road, rail, air), bio-technology, agriculture, defense, intelligent systems, heavy machines, semiconductor/nano-technology, security.

Step 2: IITs should be given the tasks of helping in the research and development, design and testing of the following highly advanced, high-tech equipment within the time-limits specified below.

1. L44 fighter planes with double the capability of F22; advanced radars and all other defense equipment like helicopter, submarine, tank, missile, warship, aircraft carrier and others, all more advanced than the current best technology – 8 years
2. 600 km/hour fast trains for making the travel from Leh/ Srinagar to Kanyakumari in 6 hours and from Amritsar to Imphal in 5 hours – 8 years
3. New air travel systems to make it possible to reach in 4 hours from Delhi to any place in the world – 8 years
4. Manned exploration/space lab for other solar systems – 10 years
5. Nuclear fusion energy – 8 years
6. Telecom optical communication switching – 5 years
7. Indian supercomputer – 5 years
8. Innovative product: cyclone prevention, weather control – 10 years
9. Indian luxury car, comfortable bus – 4 years
10. World's biggest land/space telescope – 8 years
11. Micro/nano-chips development – 4 years
12. All latest medical instruments more advanced than the current best technology – 5 years

13. All heavy industrial machines, road building machines, cranes, CNC, others – 8 years
14. All consumer electronics / home appliances – 8 years
15. Automatic massive flood/drought control system (canal/reservoir/pumping network), weather (fog/rain/storm/humidity) control system – 8 years

Step 3: After the R&D and design phase by the above R&D centers, manufacturing of all the above items should be done in India for their use in India and for international sale. The money earned by sale of these equipment should be used for the welfare of all the citizens.

Another significant requirement for all the above is proper education because education is the basis for increased employability of all the citizens. India has about 50 crores of young people who need the best education facilities at all the levels. For this, there is a huge need of the best education institutes, colleges, universities and schools for different domains. If the facilities are available and the education is provided cheaply to all the young people, there will not be any need of reservation based on castes. See chapter 10 Extraordinary Ultimate Goals for education reforms required to be implemented.

Main significant advantages

All the above items of the **HRDMP** will create crores of employment opportunities of high productivity, high-value jobs and will stop the talent drain to other countries. At the same time, it will make India an exporter of high-tech equipment instead of exporting free talent and importing the equipment at exorbitant prices, resulting in tremendous increase of the value of Indian rupee. Also, the living standard of Indians will be raised significantly.

17F

Village Transformation Programme (VTP)

Village Transformation Programme (VTP)

Following needs to be done in order to transform the villages completely for a progressive India:

1. Select 3 to 4 adjacent villages in an area of about 50 square kilometers.
2. Build new brick houses with toilet and connections for water, gas, optical broadband, road and provision for air-conditioning, for all the villagers.
3. Buy all the villager's mud-houses and offer them the new houses either to buy with easy loan if needed or on rent.
4. Build 5 primary schools with modern facilities like computer, TV screens, etc., for children; 2 medium/low skill professional schools for the young boys and girls. Provide the necessary teaching/helping staff.
5. Build 2 sport halls for yoga practice, playing indoor games like badminton, tennis, volleyball, etc.; 5 sport fields for football, hockey, etc.; 2 athletic tracks and 2 gymnasium halls; 10 outdoor tennis fields. Provide the necessary sports coaches for all the sport activities. Organize regular sports activities, events, tournaments.
6. Build 1 top sport school with necessary sports teachers.
7. Build 2 music schools for Indian and western classic music with instruments like harmonium, tabla, sitar, violin, cello, piano, etc. Provide music teachers for all the disciplines.
8. Build 1 top class hospital with ayurveda facilities, modern equipment and specialist units for different medical branches, and provide specialist doctors and staff for the hospital.
9. Make 10 crèches with trained staff to take care of the children of working parents.

10. Build housing facilities with toilet and connections for water, gas, optical broadband, road and provision for air-conditioning, for all the above-mentioned staff – teachers of primary/professional/music/sports schools, sport coaches, medical doctors/staff, etc.
11. Build 1 big shopping center.
12. Build 1 big supermarket with a modern restaurant.
13. Make 1 milk diary.
14. Build 2 medium industries, for example, for producing ayurveda products.
15. Make 10 gardens with flowers of which 2 rose gardens; 1 fun/entertainment park.
16. Make 2 disaster help centers for fire-brigade and catastrophic help.
17. Build 1 modern railway station with connection to the rail network.
18. Make road connections to all the houses, schools, sport halls, hospital, supermarket, disaster help centers, garden, fun park, railway station, offices, etc. and to adjacent villages and nearby cities.
19. Provide bus service with modern low-level floor buses serving all the housing colonies, schools, sport halls, hospital, supermarket, disaster help centers, garden, fun park, railway station, etc.
20. Make 3 underground big water tanks for rain water storage. Make big rain water receiving funnel structures with pipes connected to these tanks.
21. Build a water purification plant connected to the underground water tanks to receive the water from the underground water tank.
22. Build a pure water storage tank connected to the water purification plant to receive pure water from the water purification plant and store it.
23. Build a water distribution network to distribute the pure water from the pure water storage tank to all the houses and other buildings.
24. Appoint 13 responsible persons for the following and make offices for them.

a. Administration – birth/death registration/certificates, passport, driving license, etc.
b. Social needs – education, sports, employment, health, housing, security, pension, etc.
c. Infrastructure control – roads, transport, education, sports, hospitals, judicial help, electricity, water, gas, etc.
d. Tax
e. Police
f. Health
g. Pollution
h. Garbage
i. Traffic
j. Culture
k. Sports
l. MLA
m. General management consultant for monitoring/co-ordination

25. Make a computer database with all the villagers' data – personal, economic, education, professional, etc. to be used by the above-mentioned 13 responsible persons.
26. Provide polite, people-friendly, well-trained, well-equipped police staff equal to about 4 per cent of the population.
27. Make solar energy park for providing electricity to all the village houses and all the other buildings mentioned above.
28. Make 2 books/cd libraries and reading rooms.
29. Make 2 auditoriums of 100 to 800 seats for cultural activities and organize regular cultural/musical programmes.
30. Build 20 very clean and hygienic public toilets.
31. Provide facilities for garbage collection/disposal.
32. Provide 5 banks with free bank account and bank card for everybody.
33. Provide online payment system for all the businesses, shops, vendors – small medium and big, make all the payment by bank card obligatory, and bank withdrawal limited to Rs 1,000 max. per month for each family.
34. Organize public meetings of all the public with the elected representatives on every Saturday/Sunday for public

clarifications, discussions, grievances, improvements, suggestions, etc.

35. Integrate with all the other systems, subsystems, programms of the unique transformation programme.

18

Tasks Lists

Tasks Lists

Tasks lists at different levels – national, state, capital – have been derived based on the unique transformation programme and are presented for the whole India, Delhi, and UP state in the subsequent sub-chapters.

18A

India Programme Tasks

Example – India Programme Tasks

India transformation programme is the top-level program to be implemented at the national level. This programme has been described in the earlier chapters and has the ultimate goal of raising the living standard of all the Indians living in India by about 100 times with an aim to change the position of India from the current 135 to move in the first 10 of the international UN Human Development Index of about 190 countries.

The programme takes into account the following aspects of India: present area (about 30,50,000 sq. km), present population (about 120 crore), population density (about 300)

All the lower level programs are based on and are derived from this program.

India Transformation Programme contents:

1. Managed zones:

India will be divided into 60 thousand managed zones of approx. 50 sq. km each. For each managed zone, the following strictly monitored offices with trained staff will be established:

a. Administration – birth/death registration/ certificates, passport, driving license, etc.
b. Social needs – education, sports, employment, health, housing, security, pension, etc.
c. Infrastructure control – roads, transport, education, sports, hospitals, judicial help, electricity, water, gas, etc.
d. Tax
e. Police
f. Health
g. Pollution
h. Garbage
i. Traffic
j. Culture
k. Sports

l. MLA
m. General management consultant for monitoring/co-ordination

2. Zero corruption:

a. All the above responsible persons connected by mobile video VPN (Virtual Private Network) for strict monitoring and control

3. Citizen care:

a. All the citizens registered in a database for monitoring their social, educational, health and other needs for taking the right actions for their welfare

4. Education:

a. 6 lakh primary, 6 lakh secondary very high-quality schools
b. 6 lakh very high standard colleges
c. 1,500 universities
d. Extra-help in study for weak students
e. New: 200 IITs, 200 AIIMSs, 200 IIMs
f. 3.5 lakh medium/low-skill (technical/non-technical) professional schools
g. Crèches/schools for temporary migrant workers' children
h. Foreign/regional language classes for children
i. Yoga classes for children
j. 1.5 lakh books/cd libraries/reading rooms
k. Inter-disciplinary engineering education: chip design + mechanical/medical/.

5. Transport:

a. Much better road layout standards (West-European style) with trees, flowers, separate pedestrian, bicycle paths
b. Road construction according to new road layout standards on at least 20 per cent area of each Managed Zone
c. Extensive road network of highways, national roads and local roads

d. Much better buses of international standard
e. Much better, trained, polite, helpful bus staff
f. 5 to 10 times increase in frequency of buses according to the requirement of individual route
g. Cheaper, better taxi service
h. Replacement of 3-wheelers by small taxis
i. Replacement of manual rickshaws by motor-driven rickshaws
j. Point-to-point bus transport system for office goers reducing the private car traffic
k. Super-fast train connections for interconnection of all the national big cities: 5 hours journey from Kashmir to Kanyakumari, 5 hours from Amritsar to Imphal, etc.
l. Battery operated vehicles for inner city
m. 600 airports with all the modern infrastructure
n. 30 international airports – at least one in each state

6. Traffic:

a. 2.5 lakh underground/multistoreyed parkings of 100 to 1000 places
b. Strict traffic/driving rules
c. 6 lakh sq. km roads connecting each house/apartment to the state road network
d. 1.2 crore pedestrian crossings
e. Extensive traffic signs
f. Road markings on all the roads
g. Special traffic police with strict monitoring/training
h. Frequent & strict speed control checks
i. Frequent & strict drink control checks

7. Health:

a. 60 thousand top class hospitals
b. Free doctor house visit for 50+ health check-up/follow-up (not even in Europe)
c. Cheap medicines
d. Chemist shop/doctor available on Sunday/holiday/night
e. Effective and quick ambulance service
f. Home help for handicapped/seriously ill/old people

g. Disease prevention information pamphlets for free distribution

8. Housing:

a. Decent housing with toilet for all the families, no slums
b. Social housing for economic weaker section
c. All houses connected by road to state road network
d. 24-hours electricity, water, gas connection
e. Temporary migrant workers' housing

9. Sports:

a. 6 lakh sport clubs
b. 60 thousand top sport schools
c. 1.2 lakh sport halls for indoor games – badminton, volley ball, basketball, gymnasium
d. 60 thousand athletic tracks
e. 1.2 lakh football/hockey fields
f. 1.2 lakh tennis fields with 5 to 10 courts
g. 200 Olympic gold medals target
h. 1,200 world top badminton, tennis, table tennis players each
i. 120 world top hockey, football, volleyball, basketball, gymnasium, athletic teams each
j. 60 thousand fitness centers

10. Safety:

a. 1.2 lakh well-equipped disaster help/recovery centers
b. Emergency help at railway stations, airports, in thc whole India
c. All electric cables underground, no open naked cables anywhere
d. No open drainage holes anywhere

11. Justice:

a. 10 to 20 times increase in judicial system infrastructure, courts, judges, staff etc. for quick justice

12. Culture:

a. 2.4 lakh music schools, Indian classic (south, north, rabindra sangit)/western classic (piano, orchestra)

b. 1.2 lakh auditoriums of 100 to 800 seats
c. 60 thousand top Sitar players
d. 18 thousand Indian classic music orchestras
e. 60 thousand world top classic pianists
f. 18 thousand western classic music orchestras

13. Hygiene:

a. 60 lakh extremely clean and hygienic public toilets
b. Extremely clean roads and all public places, no garbage anywhere in open places

14. Price control:

a. 1.2 lakh cheap, big, high-quality supermarkets
b. 60 thousand milk dairies

15. Governance transparency:

a. Zero corruption and full transparency in all financial dealings/contracts

16. Environment:

a. Industrial waste disposal control
b. Vehicle emission control
c. Noise pollution control
d. 4 lakh rose/other flowers gardens
e. Massive tree plantation
f. Zero river pollution

17. Shopping:

a. 1.2 lakh big shopping centers
b. Fixed prices, compulsory price display

18. Security:

a. Increase in police for security with strict monitoring/training of police to help public, police staff 3 to 5 per cent of the population
b. Special attention for safety of women – heavy day/night patrol of women police.
c. Defense staff 3 to 5 per cent of the population
d. Judicial staff 5 per cent of the population

19. Entertainment:

a. Sports/culture TV channel
b. 12 thousand fun/entertainment parks

20. Comfort:

a. Proper scheduling of air-flights for no take-off and landing at night to reduce noise for the people living near the airports

21. Waste management:

a. Effective garbage collection/disposal
b. Better sewer system

22. Help desk:

a. Central help desk for all the problems of transport, gas, electricity, garbage collection

23. Better work conditions:

a. 40 hours per week
b. 6 lakh top quality crèches for children of working mothers

24. Old age help:

a. Top quality old age homes for helpless old people

25. Energy:

a. 50-70 per cent solar energy
b. Nuclear reactors

26. Research centers:

a. Weather control
b. Nano-technology
c. Agriculture
d. Medicine – malaria, cancer, AIDS
e. Very high speed train
f. Supercomputer
g. Telecom

h. Home appliances
i. Automation
j. Innovative products: alternative paper
k. Defense equipment
l. Medical equipment
m. Heavy machines
n. Nuclear fusion technology

27. New industries:

a. Airplane manufacturing
b. High speed train manufacturing
c. Supercomputer manufacturing
d. Custom chip design and manufacturing

28. Zero black money, zero tax evasion:

a. 3 lakh banks
b. Free bank account and bank card for everybody
c. Online payment system for all the businesses, shops, vendors – small, medium and big
d. 30 lakh Online Payment Service Centers (OPSC)
e. All payment by bank card
f. Bank withdrawal limited to Rs 1000 max per month for each family

29. Elected representatives public meetings in all the 60 thousand Managed Zones:

a. Every Saturday/Sunday for public clarifications, discussions, grievances, improvements, suggestions, etc.

30. Nutrition:

a. Zero food adulteration
b. 1.2 lakh very high-quality cheap restaurants

31. Professional migration:

a. Professional migration compensation from the immigration country

32. Water resources: Extensive canal/reservoir/umping/ purification network

Advanced, automatic zero flood/drought, zero drinking water shortage and zero river water pollution system with massive canal/reservoir/pumping/purification network for full water utilization.

A. Full water utilization and control advanced features

This modern, automated system with automatic controls, measurements and monitoring will be a unique, powerful, massive water control and utilization system. It will have the following advanced features:

i. Coverage

It will cover the following:

1. Built for about 200 to 300 rivers in India
2. Beneficial for complete 30 lakh square km area of India

ii. Infrastructure

a. Canal/reservoir/pumping/purification network infrastructure construction

Following is an approximate infrastructure requirement of the canals, reservoirs, pumps, water purification plants, etc.

1. Underground Storage tanks: about 20 thousand
2. Storage tank gates: about 50 thousand
3. Drinking water purification plants: about 20 thousand
4. Waste/drainage water purification plants: about 20 thousand
5. Canal distribution network 2 to 3 lakh square kms
6. Canal interconnection gates: about 1 to 2 lakh
7. Drinking water distribution network to all the houses: to cover about 30 crore houses/apartments/buildings

b. Measurements and monitoring network

The following is an approximate requirement of automatic measurement points and monitoring network:

1. Rainfall level measurement points: about 10 thousand
2. River water level measurement points: about 20 thousand
3. Storage tank level measurement points: about 20 thousand
4. Canal water level measurement points: about 50 thousand
5. River water purity monitoring points: about 10 thousand

18B

Delhi Programme Tasks

Example – Delhi Programme Tasks

Based on India's unique transformation program, a Delhi transformation program is formulated which is presented below

Delhi Transformation Programme:

The Delhi Transformation Programme has three levels:

1st level – India's unique transformation programme is the top-level programme to be implemented at the national level which has been presented in the earlier chapters. All the lower level programmes are based on and are derived from this programme.

2nd level – Delhi Transformation programme corresponding to the National transformation programme has the following features:

1. It is derived from the National Transformation Programme and conforms to it regarding quantitative and qualitative aspects.
2. It takes into account the following aspects of Delhi:
   a. present area (about 1,500 sq. km), present population (about 1.4 crore), population density (about 9300), estimated population after 5 years (about 2 crore)

Delhi Transformation Programme contents:

1. Managed Zones:

Delhi will be divided into 30 Managed Zones of approx. 50 sq. km each. For each managed zone, the following strictly monitored offices with trained staff will be established:

a. Social care – education, sports, employment, health, housing, security, pension, etc.

b. Administration – birth/death registration/certificates, passport, driving license, etc.
c. Infrastructure control – roads, transport, electricity, water, gas, etc.
d. Tax
e. Police
f. IIealth
g. Pollution
h. Garbage
i. Traffic
j. Culture
k. Sports
l. MLA
m. General management consultant

2. Zero corruption:

a. All the above responsible persons connected by mobile video VPN (Virtual Private Network) for strict monitoring and control.

3. Citizen care:

a. All the citizens of Delhi registered in a database for monitoring their social, educational, health and other needs for taking the right actions for their welfare.

4. Education:

a. 300 primary, 300 secondary very high-quality schools
b. 500 very high standard colleges
c. 10 universities
d. Extra-help in study for weak students
e. New: 3 IITs, 3 AIIMSs, 3 IIMs
f. 200 medium/low-skill (technical/non-technical) professional schools
g. Crèches/schools for temporary migrant workers' children
h. Foreign/regional language classes for children
i. Yoga classes for children
j. 100 books/cd libraries/reading rooms
k. Inter-disciplinary engineering education: chip design + mechanical/medical/..

5. Transport:

a. Much better road layout standards (West-European style) with trees, flowers, separate pedestrian, bicycle paths
b. Road construction according to new road layout standards on at least 20 per cent area of each Managed Zone
c. Much better buses of international standard
d. Much better, trained, polite, helpful bus staff
e. 5 to 10 times increase in frequency of buses according to the requirement of individual route
f. Cheaper, better taxi service
g. Replacement of three-wheelers by small taxis
h. Replacement of manual rickshaws by motor-driven rickshaws
i. Point-to-point bus transport system for office goers reducing the private car traffic
j. Fast train connections to nearby cities of other managed zones
k. Battery operated vehicles for inner city

6. Traffic:

a. 100 underground/multistoried parkings of 100 to 1000 places
b. Strict traffic/driving rules
c. 300 sq. km roads connecting each house/apartment to the state road network
d. 8 thousand pedestrian crossings
e. Extensive traffic signs
f. Road markings on all the roads
g. Special traffic police with strict monitoring/training
h. Frequent & strict speed control checks
i. Frequent & strict drink control checks

7. Health:

a. 30 top class hospitals
b. Free doctor house visit for 50+ health check-up/follow-up (not even in Europe)
c. Cheap medicines

d. Chemist shop/doctor available on Sunday/holiday/night
e. Effective and quick ambulance service
f. Home help for handicapped/seriously ill/old people
g. Disease prevention information pamphlets for free distribution

8. Housing:

a. Decent housing with toilet for all the families, no slums
b. 24-hours electricity, water, gas connection
c. All houses connected by road to state road network
d. Social housing for economic weak section
e. Temporary migrant workers' housing

9. Sports:

a. 100 sport clubs
b. 30 top sports schools
c. 60 sport halls for indoor games – badminton, volley ball, basketball, gymnasium
d. 30 athletic tracks
e. 60 football/hockey fields
f. 60 tennis fields with 5 to 10 courts
g. 25 Olympic gold medals
h. 25 world top badminton, tennis, table tennis players
i. 20 world top hockey, football, volleyball, basketball, gymnasium, athletic teams
j. 30 fitness centers

10. Safety:

a. 60 well-equipped disaster help/recovery centers
b. Emergency help at railway stations, airport, whole Delhi
c. All electric cables underground, no open naked cables anywhere
d. No open drainage holes anywhere

11. Justice:

a. 10 to 20 times increase in judicial system infrastructure, courts, judges, staff etc., for quick justice

12. Culture:

a. 100 music schools, Indian classic (south, north, rabindra sangit)/western classic (piano, orchestra)
b. 60 auditoriums of 100 to 800 seats
c. 30 top Sitar players
d. 10 Indian classic music orchestras
e. 30 world top classic pianists
f. 5 western classic music orchestras

13. Hygiene:

a. 3 thousand extremely clean and hygienic public toilets
b. Extremely clean roads and all public places, no garbage anywhere in open places

14. Price control:

a. 60 cheap, big, high-quality supermarkets
b. 30 milk dairies

15. Governance transparency:

a. Zero corruption and full transparency in all financial dealings/contracts

16. Environment:

a. Industrial waste disposal control
b. Vehicle emission control
c. Noise pollution control
d. 60 rose/other flowers gardens
e. Massive tree plantation
f. Zero river pollution

17. Shopping:

a. 60 big shopping centers
b. Fixed prices, compulsory price display

18. Security:

a. Increase in police for security with strict monitoring/ training of police to help public

b. Special attention for safety of women – heavy day/night patrol of women police.
c. Judicial staff 5 per cent of the population

19. Entertainment:

a. Sports/culture TV channel
b. 6 fun/entertainment parks

20. Comfort:

a. Proper scheduling of air flights for no landing and take-off at night to reduce noise for the people living near the airports

21. Waste management:

a. Effective garbage collection/disposal
b. Better sewer system

22. Help desk:

a. Central help desk for all the problems of transport, gas, electricity, garbage collection

23. Better work conditions:

a. 40 hours per week
b. 300 top quality crèches for children of working mothers

24. Old age help:

a. Top quality old age homes for helpless old people

25. Energy:

a. 50–70 per cent solar energy

26. Research centers:

a. Weather control
b. Nano-technology
c. Agriculture
d. Medicine – malaria, cancer, AIDS

e. Very high speed train
f. Supercomputer
g. Telecom
h. Home appliances
i. Automation
j. Innovative products: alternative paper
k. Defense equipment
l. Medical equipment
m. Heavy machines
n. Nuclear fusion technology

27. Nutrition:

a. Zero food adulteration
b. 60 very high-quality cheap restaurants

28. Zero black money, zero tax evasion:

a. 1500 banks
b. Free bank account and bank card for everybody
c. Online payment system for all the businesses, shops, vendors – small, medium and big
d. 1500 lakh Online Payment Service Centers (OPSC)
e. All payment by bank card
f. Bank withdrawal limited to Rs 1000 max per month for each family

29. Elected representatives public meetings in all the 30 Managed Zones:

a. Every Saturday/Sunday for public clarifications, discussions, grievances, improvements, suggestions, etc.

3rd level – MCD programme derived from the Delhi Transformation Programme according to MCD domain/scope of work. MCD will have to be submerged with the managed zones and restructured accordingly.

18C

UP Programme Tasks

Example – UP Programme Tasks

Uttar Pradesh Programme:

UP Programme has 2 levels:

1st level – India's unique transformation programme is the top-level programme to be implemented at the national level which has been presented in the earlier chapters. All the lower level programmes are based on and are derived from this programme.

2nd level – UP Transformation programme corresponding to the National transformation programme has the following features:

1. It is derived from the National Transformation Programme and conforms to it regarding quantitative and qualitative aspects.
2. It takes into account the following aspects of UP:
   a. present area (about 2,50,000 sq. km), present population (about 21 crore), population density (about 830)

UP Transformation Programme contents:

1. Managed zones:

UP will be divided into 5 thousand managed zones of approx. 50 sq. km each. For each managed zone, the following strictly monitored offices with trained staff will be established:

a. Administration – birth/death registration/certificates, passport, driving license, etc.
b. Social needs – education, sports, employment, health, housing, security, pension, etc.
c. Infrastructure control – roads, transport, education, sports, hospitals, judicial help, electricity, water, gas, etc.
d. Tax

e. Police
f. Health
g. Pollution
h. Garbage
i. Traffic
j. Culture
k. Sports
l. MLA
m. General management consultant for monitoring/co-ordination

2. Zero corruption:

a. All the above responsible persons connected by mobile video VPN (Virtual Private Network for strict monitoring and control)

3. Citizen care:

a. All the citizens registered in a database for monitoring their social, educational, health and other needs for taking the right actions for their welfare

4. Education:

a. 50 thousand primary, 50 thousand secondary very high-quality schools
b. 50 thousand very high standard colleges
c. 150 universities
d. Extra-help in study for weak students
e. New: 30 IITs, 30 AIIMSs, 30 IIMs
f. 35 thousand medium/low-skill (technical/non-technical) professional schools
g. Crèches/schools for temporary migrant worker's children
h. Foreign/regional language classes for children
i. Yoga classes for children
j. 15 thousand books/cd libraries/reading rooms
k. Inter-disciplinary engineering education: chip design + mechanical/medical/..

5. Transport:

a. Much better road layout standards (West-European style) with trees, flowers, separate pedestrian, bicycle paths
b. Road construction according to new road layout standards on at least 20 per cent area of each Managed Zone
c. Extensive road network of highways, national roads and local roads
d. Much better buses of international standard
e. Much better, trained, polite, helpful bus staff
f. 5 to 10 times increase in frequency of buses according to the requirement of individual routes
g. Cheaper, better taxi service
h. Replacement of three-wheelers by small taxis
i. Replacement of manual rickshaws by motor-driven rickshaws
j. Point-to-point bus transport system for office goers reducing the private car traffic
k. Super-fast train connections for interconnection of UP cities and of UP cities to other national big cities: Mirzapur to Saharanpur – 2 hours, Lucknow to Delhi – 2 hours, Lucknow to Mumbai – 6 hours, Lucknow to Chennai – 6 hours, Lucknow to Kolkata – 3 hours, etc.
l. Battery operated vehicles for inner city
m. 50 airports with all the modern infrastructure
n. 3 international airports – Lucknow, Varanasi, Jhansi

6. Traffic:

a. 20 thousand underground/multistoried parking of 100 to 1000 places
b. Strict traffic/driving rules
c. 50 thousand sq. km roads connecting each house/ apartment to the state road network
d. 10 lakh pedestrian crossings
e. Extensive traffic signs
f. Road markings on all the roads
g. Special traffic police with strict monitoring/training
h. Frequent & strict speed control checks
i. Frequent & strict drink control checks

7. Health:

a. 5 thousand top class hospitals

b. Free doctor house visit for 50+ health check-up/follow-up (not even in Europe)
c. Cheap medicines
d. Chemist shop/doctor available on Sunday/holiday/night
e. Effective and quick ambulance service
f. Home help for handicapped/seriously ill/old people
g. Disease prevention information pamphlets for free distribution

8. Housing:

a. Decent housing with toilet for all the families, no slums
b. Social housing for economic weak section
c. All houses connected by road to state road network
d. 24-hours electricity, water, gas connection
e. Temporary migrant worker's housing

9. Sports:

a. 50 thousand sport clubs
b. 5 thousand top sport schools
c. 10 thousand sport halls for indoor games – badminton, volley ball, basketball, gymnasium
d. 5 thousand athletic tracks
e. 10 thousand football/hockey fields
f. 10 thousand tennis fields with 5 to 10 courts
g. 100 Olympic gold medals
h. 100 world top badminton, tennis, table tennis players each
i. 50 world top hockey, football, volleyball, basketball, gymnasium, athletic teams
j. 5 thousand fitness centers

10. Safety:

a. 10 thousand well-equipped disaster help/recovery centers
b. Emergency help at railway stations, airport, whole UP
c. All electric cables underground, no open naked cables anywhere
d. No open drainage holes anywhere

11. Justice:

a. 10 to 20 times increase in judicial system infrastructure, courts, judges, staff etc., for quick justice

12. Culture:

a. 20 thousand music schools, Indian classic (south, north, rabindra sangit)/western classic (piano, orchestra)
b. 20 thousand auditoriums of 100 to 800 seats
c. 5 thousand top Sitar players
d. 1,500 Indian classic music orchestras
e. 5 thousand world top classic pianists
f. 1,500 western classic music orchestras

13. Hygiene:

a. 5 lakh extremely clean and hygienic public toilets
b. Extremely clean roads and all public places, no garbage anywhere in open places

14. Price control:

a. 10 thousand cheap, big, high-quality supermarkets
b. 5 thousand milk dairies

15. Governance transparency:

a. Zero corruption and full transparency in all financial dealings/contracts

16. Environment:

a. Industrial waste disposal control
b. Vehicle emission control
c. Noise pollution control
d. 30 thousand rose/other flowers gardens
e. Massive tree plantation
f. Zero river pollution

17. Shopping:

a. 10 thousand big shopping centers
b. Fixed prices, compulsory price display

18. Security:

a. Increase in police for security with strict monitoring/ training of police to help public, police staff 3 to 5 per cent of the population
b. Special attention for safety of women – heavy day/night patrol of women police.
c. Judicial staff 5 per cent of the population

19. Entertainment:

a. Sports/culture TV channel
b. 1 thousand fun/entertainment parks

20. Comfort:

a. Proper scheduling of air flights for no landing and take-off at night to reduce noise for the people living near the airports

21. Waste management:

a. Effective garbage collection/disposal
b. Better sewer system

22. Help desk:

a. Central help desk for all the problems of transport, gas, electricity, garbage collection

23. Better work conditions:

a. 40 hours per week
b. 50 thousand top quality crèches for children of working mothers

24. Old age help:

a. Top quality old age homes for helpless old people

25. Energy:

a. 50-70 per cent solar energy
b. Nuclear reactors

26. Research centers:

a. Weather control
b. Nano-technology
c. Agriculture
d. Medicine – malaria, cancer, AIDS
e. Very high speed train
f. Supercomputer
g. Telecom
h. Home appliances
i. Automation
j. Innovative products – alternative paper
k. Defense equipment
l. Medical equipment
m. Heavy machines
n. Nuclear fusion technology

27. New industries:

a. Airplane manufacturing
b. High speed train manufacturing
c. Supercomputer manufacturing
d. Custom chip design and manufacturing

28. Zero black money, zero tax evasion:

a. 25 thousand banks
b. Free bank account and bank card for everybody
c. Online payment system for all the businesses, shops, vendors - small, medium and big.
d. 2.5 lakh Online Payment Service Centers (OPSC)
e. All payment by bank card
f. Bank withdrawal limited to Rs 1000 max per month for each family

29. Elected representatives public meetings in all the 5 thousand Managed Zones:

a. Every Saturday/Sunday for public clarifications, discussions, grievances, improvements, suggestions, etc.

30. Nutrition:

a. Zero food adulteration
b. 10 thousand Very high-quality cheap restaurants

31. Water resources: Extensive canal/reservoir/pumping/purification network

Advanced, automatic zero flood/drought, zero drinking water shortage and zero river water pollution system with massive canal/reservoir/pumping/purification network for full water utilization.

A. Full water utilization and control advanced features

This modern, automated system with automatic controls, measurements and monitoring will be a unique, powerful, massive water control and utilization system. It will have the following advanced features:

i. Coverage

It will cover the following:

1. Built for about 20 to 30 rivers in UP
2. Beneficial for complete 2.5 lakh square km area of UP

ii. infrastructure construction

a. Canal/reservoir/pumping/purification network infrastructure construction

Following is an approximate infrastructure requirement of the canals, reservoirs, pumps, water purification plants, etc.

1. Underground Storage tanks: about 2 thousand
2. Storage tank gates: about 5 thousand
3. Drinking water purification plants: about 2 thousand
4. Waste/drainage water purification plants: about 2 thousand
5. Canal distribution network 20 to 30 thousand square kms
6. Canal interconnection gates: about 10 to 20 thousand
7. Drinking water distribution network to all the houses: to cover about 3 crore houses/apartments/buildings

b. Measurements and monitoring network

The following is an approximate requirement of automatic

measurement and monitoring network:

1. Rainfall level measurement points: about 1 thousand
2. River water level measurement points: about 2 thousand
3. Storage tank level measurement points: about 2 thousand
4. Canal water level measurement points: about 5 thousand
5. River water purity monitoring points: about 1 thousand

Appendix 1

Estimation of Job Opportunities

Estimation of Job Opportunities

Some simple calculations to give an idea of the job opportunities that will be available by the implementation of the unique transformation programme all over India are provided below. All the numbers are approximate estimations and can vary according to the situation.

Applicable for about 60 thousand managed zones (l = lakh persons, cr = crore persons):

managed zone management	24 l
sport teachers	6 l
music teachers	6 l
professional school teachers	6 l
hospital	18 l
supermarket	18 l
construction for infrastructure	18 l
primary school teachers	18 l
secondary school teachers	18 l
college/university professors	12 l
dairy	6 l
restaurant	12 l
garden/park	20 l

transport services	6 l
crèche	12 l
library	6 l
parking	2 l
disaster/recovery centre	6 l
justice system	6 l
toilets	40 l
general cleanliness	1 cr
bank for on-line payment system	20 l
on-line payment service center staff	20 l
research centers	1 l
heavy industries	4 l
police	4 cr
defense	4 cr
sub-total =	12 cr 5 l
indirect employment	1 cr
total =	13 cr 5 l

Hence, according to the rough estimation, about 13 crore jobs can be created all over the nation by the implementation of the unique transformation programme.

List of Acronyms Used

AIDS	Acquired Immune Deficiency Syndrome
AIIMS	All India Institute of Medical Sciences
AZFDS	Automatic Zero Flood/Drought System
CCS	Citizen Complaint Sub-system
CDB	Citizen Database
CDPS	Citizen Democratic Participation System
CNC	Computer Numerical Control (machine)
CRRS	Citizens Requirements Request Sub-system
EMS	Execution, Monitoring and Control System
ES	Execution Sub-system
HDI	Human Development Index
HRDMP	Home R&D, Design and Manufacturing Programme
IIM	Indian Institute of Management
IIT	Indian Institute of Technology
IT	Information Technology
MCD	Municipal Corporation of Delhi
MCS	Monitoring and Control Sub-system
MLA	Member of Legislative Assembly
MP	Member of Parliament
MVVS	Mobile Video VPN Sub-system
OPN	On-line Payment Network
OPSC	On-line Payment Service center
OPT	On-line Payment Terminal
R&D	Research and Development
UN	United Nations
UNICEF	United Nations Children's Fund
UP	Uttar Pradesh

VPN	Virtual Private Network
VTP	Village Transformation Programme
WPMFAS	Weekly Public Meeting Feedback and Action Sub-system
ZBTS	Zero Black money and Zero Tax-evasion System

Index